CAN YOU SEE US NOW?

Cheryl Benton

Copyright © 2018 Cheryl Benton

All rights reserved.

ISBN-13: 978-0692054048
ISBN-10: 0692054049

The Three Tomatoes Publishing
New York
www.thethreetomatoes.com

DEDICATION

This book is dedicated to every woman who has ever felt
invisible.

And to Fergus O'Daly, our dear friend and mentor,
who inspired us and made us laugh, and coined
the term The Three Tomatoes.
We miss you.

1

BECOMING INVISIBLE

It felt great being inside the air-conditioned bar at Balthazar. Suzy was glad she had arrived early and grabbed three stools at the end of the bar. She hated these damned hot and humid days. And throw in the hot flashes and it made a bad day worse. At least she could cool down a bit before Madge and Trish arrived. This was their usual martini meet up before their monthly dinner with a group of friends who laughingly call themselves the Ripe Tomatoes.

She ordered a dirty martini from the very cute bartender with a crooked smile, perfect teeth, and sandy hair with a little stray piece that almost touched his baby blues. Another aspiring actor. Damn, he looks so young. But then so do the cops and firefighters these days. Not to mention everyone in the ad agency she works for, Secret Agent. The name alone tells you it's another "trendy" agency where anyone over forty starts to feel like a dinosaur.

She was looking forward to shedding her bad day with her two best pals. They'd all been friends since their first jobs with a big New York City ad agency right out of college, and there wasn't much they didn't know about each other or hadn't shared about their lives. They still laugh about their first apartment, a one-bedroom with twin beds and a pullout couch. Whichever one arrived home the latest got the couch. They had started their martini meet up tradition back then because it seemed like such a "grownup" drink.

Suzy had stayed in the advertising business, although she was having regrets about that now. Madge had gone into TV journalism, another cutthroat industry, and Trish had married a wealthy hedge fund guy and had the luxury of owning an art gallery, mostly for the fun of it.

They had been bridesmaids at each other's weddings. Suzy was the first to get married, and was still with Ken, a corporate attorney. They had two children in quick succession, their daughter, Keri, and son, Ian. After he was born, they moved out of the city to Bronxville. They wanted the kids raised in the suburbs and Bronxville was an easy commute to the city since both she and Ken worked there.

Trish married Michael a couple of years later, and their marriage was still intact too. Trish would have loved to have children, but it wasn't in the cards.

Madge didn't get married until she was almost forty, and the marriage didn't last much longer than the wedding reception. Seems he cheated on their honeymoon!

Now here they were more than twenty-five years later. They still looked damned good — Suzy, with her blonde highlighted hair, was tall and still trim (although lately she felt her middle was expanding). Madge was a dramatic-looking brunette who worked out all the time and had the arms to prove it. Trish was a petite redhead, who was into organic food, and holistic and healthy anything and everything.

Ahh...Sandy Blue Eyes put the martini in front of her. She took the first sip and already felt better. On her second sip, two beautiful models floated in and took seats at the center of the bar. Sandy Blue Eyes made a mad dash to grant them their every wish with his most ingratiating crooked smile.

On her third sip, Madge and Trish saddled up to the bar.

"Hello, darling...it's so fucking hot my panties are melting," Madge said as she air-kissed Suzy.

Trish, looking cool as a cucumber in a little white linen dress with spaghetti straps and four-inch wedge sandals (how did she always look so damn perfect?), sat in between them. "Martinis...just what we need." She gave a little nod in the direction of Sandy Blue Eyes that went unnoticed because he was too busy impressing the models with his mint muddling skills for the mojitos they had ordered.

"Oh, bartender," Madge shouted in her most sultry voice, which also went unnoticed, prompting Madge to get up and interrupt the mint muddling reverie to order the martinis.

"Fuck — we've just become invisible. And how was your day, darlings?" said Madge as the errant martinis made their way to their end of the bar.

Suzy raised her glass to cheer her friends. "Oh, I had another lovely day in ad agency paradise being the oldest person in the conference room, and if that isn't bad enough, I had a hot flash just as I was presenting to the client and then a brain freeze."

"Have you been taking your black cohosh and exercising more?"

"No, Trish, I'm happy I find time to brush my teeth in the morning."

Trish rolled her eyes.

"My day was hell too," said Madge. "The rumor is that the network is thinking of moving me from the morning show to the midday 'entertainment' spot. *Midday*, for Christ's sake, who watches the midday news? I know they've got that thirtysomething former beauty queen with a law degree from Harvard already lined up. I think the handwriting is on the wall. You're so lucky you own your own art gallery, Trish, and don't have to worry about being usurped by an overachieving, corporate ladder-climbing charmer who has men drooling on themselves."

"I'm sure it's just this wretched heat getting both of you down," said Trish always the optimist of the trio. "Let's focus on something fun, like planning Suzy's big 5-0 birthday."

"Oh God, do not say that out loud. There is no way I am celebrating this birthday. I've already told Ken and the kids *not* to plan anything. And I swear I'll kill anyone who tries to come up with a surprise party. I plan to take to my bed that day, eat bonbons, and watch old movies. And *do not* mention this to the Tomatoes tonight. I just can't deal."

"At least you have a husband and kids. Not that I miss that cheating ex-husband of mine, but dating is so exhausting. And I haven't felt attracted to anyone in so long, my vagina will probably dry up like a prune." And with that Madge downed the entire martini in one gulp.

"Yikes, what's happened to us?" said Trish. "Our girls' nights out used to be fun. We'd flirt with the bartender, drink those drinks like the models are having, and laugh...a lot."

"Well that was before menopause, hot flashes, and unsolicited membership cards from AARP," replied Suzy. "And where the hell is Sandy Blue Eyes with our check?"

2

DINNER AND THE BILLIONAIRE

Oh God, here we go again, thought Suzy. Ordering dinner for their monthly Ripe Tomatoes gathering would try the patience of Job, never mind a seasoned New York City waiter. "Is the salmon organic? What do you have that's gluten free? I'm on a fat-free, low-carb diet. Is the chicken free-range? Can you do the French onion soup without the cheese? I'm lactose intolerant. And please bring my ice tea with an extra glass of ice and three lemon slices on the side cut in quarters."

Finally, dinner was ordered, drinks arrived, and the group settled down to sharing what's on their minds. The Ripe Tomatoes dinners were started three years earlier by their friend Hope, a bigger than life Broadway producer to bring together her "brilliant and fabulous" friends to talk about anything they wanted to with the promise that whatever happened at the table, stayed at the table.

She selected twelve very accomplished professional women with careers in media, advertising, arts, theater, and other fields that make New York City a magnet for the best and brightest. Hope was the only one who knew all of them, and had an uncanny ability to select just the right people. Well almost. A couple of the originals were never invited back because they couldn't keep their lips zipped, and they ended up on Hope's enemy list. Fortunately, there was no shortage of brilliant and fabulous ladies in New York City, and the two loose-lipped ones were soon replaced.

It was around their third dinner together when their usual waiter, who prided himself on having been at this iconic Broadway restaurant for over forty years, looked at them appreciatively and said, "This is a group of hot tomatoes."

When he left the table, Trish was the first to ask, "What's a tomato?"

Celeste, a best-selling romance novelist, and still stunningly beautiful at seventy-four, laughed and said, "Well in my day, that's what guys called a savvy, sexy woman of a 'certain age' who knows her way around a man and a martini too, so I'd say we should take that as a compliment."

"Well this is certainly a group of ripe tomatoes," chuckled Hope. And the name stuck. Over the past three years, the Ripe Tomatoes had bonded into a loyal and supportive group who truly had each other's backs.

All twelve tomatoes happened to be at dinner tonight, a rarity since one or two usually had a conflict at the last minute.

"Thanks for getting us the alcove table, Hope — at least I can hear what everyone is saying. I find myself simply smiling at most group dinners these day."

They all nodded in agreement at Arlene's comment. As usual, Arlene, the editor of a well-known fashion magazine, looked elegant. "So how's the new show going?" she asked Hope.

"Well we still need another five hundred thousand dollars before production starts. And it didn't help that Catherine Dubois was a no-show at this week's reading. I was counting on her for two hundred thousand dollars and I swear if I find Ellen Martin has sabotaged me again I'll knock her off her stilettos faster than you can say Jimmy Choo."

"You know Ellen will be at the library fund-raiser in the fall, so be prepared," said Mimi, a Tony Award-winning actress. "Speaking of which, I had a thoroughly depressing afternoon at Saks previewing the fall cocktail dresses. I couldn't find anything to wear that doesn't end at my derriere, or plunge down to my navel. Does this town not realize we're not all size zero twentysomethings? It's all your fault, Arlene," she said jokingly.

There were familiar nods of agreement around the table. And they were all glad that Mimi had diverted the conversation because they knew Hope was heading for a rant about Ellen, especially since some of them were friends with Ellen too, a fact that Hope considered almost treasonous.

The conversation, like always, eventually got around to men — finding them, leaving them, and sex or lack of sex. And when they get to this part of the evening, they always love when Celeste holds them in rapt attention with her latest dating adventures. While Madge and Hope had many online dating disasters, Celeste had somehow attracted a bevy of successful men who all fell in love with her. But things never quite work out — the retired judge drank too much, the wealthy retired fast-food franchise owner wanted her to retire and move to a golf community in Florida. But still, her announcement at dinner was a surprise.

"Okay, Tomatoes, let me tell you something. I'm dating someone fabulous," Celeste pronounced.

"And that's news?" said Madge. "You're always dating someone fabulous. Which dating site did you meet this guy on?"

"Actually, I'm giving up on online dating because I'm just not finding the right kind of men. A couple of weeks ago I chatted for a while with the adorable new young rabbi at my synagogue. I told him I'd really like to find love again, but haven't had much success since my husband died. And to my utter surprise, he said one of his congregants is a wonderful 'older' gentleman who lost his wife a couple of years ago, and he would love to meet the right woman and even marry again. He asked if I'd like him to arrange an introduction.

"And you know, ladies," Celeste continued, "I never say no. Mr. B picked me up for our first date in his limo, and yes, it's his own private limo with a driver he's had for years. I told him I'd come downstairs and when I walked out, there he was waiting for me in the lobby and his driver was holding the door open. And off we went to Le Cirque. It was an incredible evening. Sirio even stopped by our table for a chat. Well let me tell you — Mr. B is the most interesting man I have ever met, and one of the most attentive. We've had five dates in two weeks, including last weekend when we traveled in his private jet to his estate in Costa Rica — one of three homes he owns, including the most fabulous apartment overlooking Central Park. But I'm not sure if I should continue seeing him."

"Why not?" they all screamed in unison.

"Well turns out when my rabbi said he was an 'older' man he meant really older. Mr. B is ninety-two years old, but he's so vital you'd never know it. But still, do I want to get involved with someone who's that old?"

What ensued was a wonderful and lively debate — yes of course you should continue dating him, maybe he'll leave you his money (although Celeste doesn't need his money). No, are you crazy? You could be dating guys twenty years younger than yourself the way you look.

The evening was the perfect anecdote to Suzy's hellish day and by the time she got home, a little tipsy, she gently removed the remote control from Ken's hand where he had fallen asleep while watching *Law & Order* in bed, kissed the top of his head, and climbed into bed grateful she wasn't single, but with visions of billionaires, estates, and private jets whirling in her head.

3

THE AGENCY

Suzy strolled into her office — one of those wide-open design spaces that management thinks makes them look cool where everyone sits out in the open — and common space areas include a pool table, a chess set with life-size pawns, and video games. And then there's the lounge cafeteria area with its own Starbucks barista, and a chef who makes omelets to order. All this to keep the junior employees happy that they get to spend twelve hours a day in this fun space and impress clients with how cool and creative they are.

Suzy grabbed a cappuccino and headed to one of the few actual offices in the agency allotted to directors and above, although it was a fishbowl that offered no privacy, unless you closed the shades that automatically descended with the push of a button. But of course, then everyone would get paranoid wondering who would be fired next, or think you were having wanton sex on the desk. "Hmmm...not such a bad thing for them to think," thought Suzy.

No sooner had she sat down when she got a two-paragraph text from Ryan, her thirty-five-year-old boss who is CEO of the agency, asking her how the meeting went with Arpello Perfume, one of their newest clients. It always peeved Suzy to get a text from Ryan when his office was literally across the way and she could see the top of his head as he was texting her. She picked up her coffee and walked the twenty feet to his office.

Ryan looked up. "Hey, Suzy, I just texted you."

Yes, I know, I thought I'd take the two-second stroll to your office so we can actually talk in person about it, was what Suzy wanted to reply. Instead she said, "Yeah, do you have a few minutes to chat about it?"

"Sure, have a seat." His head was down and he was back to texting.

"Well, I've been thinking. I know Arpello hired us because they want to turn themselves into a hip perfume brand for millennials, but I think that's the wrong strategy."

"Wrong? What they've got now is an ancient brand that my grandma wears. If we don't rebrand them, their audience will be dead for Christ's sake," he spewed without ever looking up from his iPhone.

"Actually, Ryan, there are a lot of women out there who know the brand and have fond memories of wearing it on first dates, their first prom, their first kiss. Those women are all now over forty-five,

13

but I think if we reposition the brand for them, and capitalize on the nostalgia, we can capture a really important market."

Without ever lifting his head and thumbs moving at lightning speed, Ryan said, dripping with sarcasm, "Suzy, have you lost it? No one wants to market perfume to old women. What would our message be? The perfume for menopausal women with dried-up vaginas? Forget it. This brand needs to go young, and that's what we're going to do."

"Got it, chief." Suzy left steaming and this time it wasn't the hot flashes.

4

THE NETWORK

"So, what do we know about this guy's personal life? Does he even have one?" Madge queried the team gathered around the table preparing for her big interview segment on Sunday night's *That's All, Folks*, the network's recently launched news and entertainment magazine. She'd be interviewing Jason Madison, the reclusive billionaire founder of the Internet's latest social app called Snazzed, which had overtaken Instagram and Snapchat as the next big thing with millennials.

"Well, he's not your typical Internet geek," Jamie said, pointing out photos of the guy at company shareholder meetings. "The guy is movie star good-looking, and actually finished Harvard while he was developing Snazzed."

"And every gorgeous female and male model seems to have thrown themselves at him," Cali chimed in. "Not to mention some of the biggest pop stars in the business today, but it appears he just brushes them off."

"But there's a rumor he was in love with one of his Harvard professors, and she died of cancer. That seems to be when he became so reclusive and started spending most of his time on his two-hundred-acre farm in Vermont," added Kyle, showing aerial photos of the land. "He has a huge office loft in SoHo, which includes his penthouse home, but he rarely spends much time in New York City. So it's a big deal he's agreed to do the interview from his office, and an even bigger deal that he's agreed to a preinterview today. We have a car picking you up in half an hour, and he just wants you there, no entourage."

As the car wove its way in and out of New York City traffic, Madge reviewed her notes. She wanted to get a sense of this guy before the on-air interview, and hopefully put him at ease so he'd be more candid with his answers. Madge prided herself on the ability to get her subjects to really open up on air as if it were just a one-on-one conversation and not being shared with millions. She made her way out of the car and up to the second floor of the loft with its soaring ceilings, beautiful wood floors, and employees sitting on couches, benches, and floor cushions with their laptops like it's a college dorm. Just as she was looking for a receptionist or someone to guide her to the big boss, a towering man stood up from a couch in the corner of the room and slowly approached her.

"I'm Jason Madison," he said with an outreached hand. And Madge found herself gazing into one of the most beautiful pair of blue eyes she'd ever seen. "And I'm Madge Thompson," she replied.

"Yes, that I know," replied Jason. "Let's go up one more flight to the conference area. It's quieter there." And with that they proceeded up the spiral staircase in the middle of the loft to the next landing, which had several small round tables with comfortable chairs, and great views of Manhattan from all directions.

Jason pulled out one of the chairs for her and sat opposite her.

"Thanks for agreeing to a premeet, Jason. I find that if we get to know each other a bit before we film and talk about some of the areas that our viewers would be interested in learning about, that makes for a better interview. So may I ask you a few questions?" Madge preferred not to take notes in these sessions but to establish a connection, and she was praying she'd remember his answers because it would be really easy to get lost in those eyes.

"So, you grew up outside of Boston. What was that like?"

Jason told her about his dad who was in the tech business, and his mom who was an artist and quite well-known in the area for her paintings that captured Boston life. His kid sister breeds horses. He was a smart kid, but never got good grades because school bored him. He did well in football, but it was discovering the robotics lab in high school that turned things around for him. He created a robot that could play chess. That and his nearly perfect SAT scores got him into Harvard. It was during his sophomore year that the idea for what eventually became Snazzed was born. But unlike many of his Internet rivals, instead of dropping out of school, he developed Snazzed in his spare time. And by the time he did graduate, he had a powerful elevator pitch that had VCs clamoring to invest. And the rest, as they say, became history.

Jason's stories were wonderful. He was articulate, self-effacing, with a great sense of humor and a really dazzling smile. Until Madge asked the last question.

"Jason, I heard you had your own version of *Love Story* while you were at Harvard. That must have been very sad."

A veil came over Jason and his whole demeanor changed. "I *do not* discuss my personal life with anyone, and if you proceed in that direction for the interview count me out." He then stood, while saying, "I think we're done for the day."

"Jason...please...I'm sorry I overstepped. This is one of the reasons I like to do these preinterviews so that we establish the boundaries. Now I know not to go there."

"Fine," he said brusquely. "My assistant will work with your team to get anything else you need for the interview later this week," and with that he was gone.

Back in the car, Madge figured it was late enough in the day that she'd just head home, when her cell phone rang. It was Martha, the assistant to Jack Feldy, head of the network and producer of *That's All, Folks*.

"Hi, Madge, Jack would like to see you in his office at 6:00 p.m. today. Does that work for you?"

When Jack Feldy wants a meeting with you, you certainly do not say, "I'm heading home for the day."

"Of course. I'm in a car heading uptown now, and traffic permitting should be there on time." Something about this call wasn't feeling right.

Martha cheerfully greeted her when she arrived and told her Jack was waiting for her. Madge always dreaded conversations in his office. She took a deep breath and walked in.

"Madge, Madge, great job this morning with the segment on 'Dressing Your Age.' Have a seat. Would you like a glass of wine or a shot of something?" Jack asked as he poured himself a single malt scotch.

"No, I'm good. Thanks."

"Well then, let's just get to the reason I called you in here. As you know we're trying to give our up-and-coming talent more high-profile opportunities, and the interview with Jason Madison would be perfect for Heather Stone."

Madge looked at Jack incredulously. "I've been working on this interview for three weeks, and I just left Jason's office and we had a great preinterview. I don't understand." Madge realized her voice was now going up an octave and she'd have to tone it back down.

"Listen, Madge. Snazzed is a story for millennials. Hell, I don't even know what it does except my grandkids are addicted. We're trying to attract a younger audience, and this is a story that could get their attention. And having a millennial do the interview, not to mention that she went to Harvard too, could really give the story more punch. So that's all, folks." That was Jack's signature "get the hell out of my office line" and how the show got its name.

With that Madge lowered her voice an octave and said, "Well, Jack, I don't really agree with this approach, but you know I'm a team player." And with all the dignity she could muster, she slowly walked out of his office.

And immediately made a beeline to the ladies' room, where after checking that it was empty, she started kicking the door of a stall, not even thinking about the damage to her Manolos, while shouting, *"Fuck, fuck, fuck!"*

5

AN IDEA IS BORN

It was time again for dinner with the Ripe Tomatoes. Madge suggested Suzy and Trish meet her at the Friars Club, where she was a member. This was a bar where they'd actually bring down the average age, and after this past week, Madge was definitely in need of feeling "youngish" again. Plus, it was quiet, and the bartender knew how to make a perfect martini. They settled into a quiet corner table in the bar area.

"Let me ask you both a question," Suzy said as they settled in with their drinks. "You can be my focus group of two. Do you remember Arpello Perfume?"

"Of course," they answered in unison.

"Well, tell me your thoughts and memories associated with it."

"I loved the guy in their ads. It was like he was looking just at me and I would have given it up for him in a second," said Madge.

"Oh, me too," said Trish. "It was my fourteenth birthday and my father gave me a bottle. It was the first time I felt grownup. And it had a wonderful distinctive fragrance that I still remember — a light scent with vanilla tones — but not at all overpowering."

"Yes, that's right," said Madge. "I remember the scent, and vanilla always makes me think of the first time I let a guy get to third base. What the heck ever happened to it anyway?"

"Well, it's still around, but hanging on by a thread. Their twentysomething marketing manager thinks it can become a hip brand marketed to millennials, and our agency has that assignment. But I really think that will be a disaster. My thought is it could be remarketed to our generation as a retro brand, recapturing those memories of our youth. But my twelve-year-old CEO put the kibosh on that idea as only for women with dried up vaginas."

"Talk about having a boss that makes you feel irrelevant, I lost my big interview with Jason Madison to that conniving little bitch, Heather Stone. Jack positioned it to me as 'giving the young talent a chance to be showcased.' I don't know how much more of this I can stand. I'd love to just walk out the door," said Madge. "But maybe that's the martini talking."

Trish, always the booster club, said, "Madge, I saw that interview and Heather was fawning all over Jason like a teenage girl. And when she asked him about the professor he was in love with, you could see him freeze on the air. It was embarrassing to watch. She doesn't come close to filling your Jimmy Choos. But, oh my God, I just realized something...Jason reminds me of the Arpello guy — maybe you can get him to be the face of the brand. You'd appeal to us and maybe the millennials too."

"Great idea," said Suzy, "but I'd have to buy the brand myself to do that. The latest round of creative features a reality star, known only for her big butt and sex tape, and her rap artist husband practically doing it in an elevator with rap music blaring in the background."

"Hmmm...now here's a martini-inspired thought," said Madge. "Maybe we should start a company that's all about women like us who refuse to be marginalized or invisible."

Suzy raised her martini glass, "Well, let's drink to that. We could call it The Three Tomatoes...for grownup women."

6

ANOTHER DINNER

They were all glad that Celeste had joined them for dinner. After a whirlwind three-month romance with her ninety-two-year-old billionaire, he died in her arms at his Costa Rica estate.

"Of course, intellectually I knew this would happen, but I still wasn't prepared. He was so vital up to the very end that I was just shocked. But I think he knew. In fact, the night before, he told me that I had brought such great joy into his life again, and he wanted to acknowledge that with a five-hundred-thousand-dollar check, as a gift. I said let's discuss this when we get back to New York. And then the next day he was gone."

"How are you feeling now?" Hope gently asked.

"I'm still sad at the loss, but so glad to have experienced these past three months." Celeste paused and then added, "And I learned if someone offers you a half million dollars, shut up and take it. That's my only regret."

They all enjoyed a good laugh at that, but they could still see the real sadness in Celeste's eyes, and it wasn't just about the money.

"Well, this may not be good timing with Celeste still in mourning," said Hope, "but I can't hold it in any longer. I've met someone."

The group immediately started firing questions at her — who, what, how, and have they done "it" yet.

"We've had several wonderful dates, which were really all-day events that went into the evening. And no, we haven't gotten to 'it' yet. My gyno says he must 'first prepare the vagina' when I'm ready." That got a huge laugh that had the entire restaurant looking their way.

"He's about my age, very good-looking and a health nut — so there goes my nightly bag of Doritos. He's in the health industry and we have a lot in common. So far so good. In fact, I'm thinking of bringing him to the library benefit, so you'll get to meet him."

They raised their glasses in cheers.

They were all happy that Marilyn had joined them this evening too. She recently went through a very high-profile divorce that made the front page of the *New York Post* for a month — mostly though because she was feeding them the juicy details of the story. Marilyn's family owns one of the most iconic restaurants in New York City, and her husband of twenty-five years was running it. Marilyn had bemoaned for years that he'd never go out at night with her because he was always too tired from running the restaurant, so she always relied on the company of her girlfriends. Turns out he relied on the company of his girlfriends too, since he had several he was chasing around during the day. As Marilyn, said, "It explained all those exhausted nights."

"So, ladies, I was reading about this big Rejuvenation & Reinvention Summit that's coming up next month. I think it might be just what I need. Anyone want to join me there?" asked Marilyn.

"Well," said Suzy, "I don't know that I need to reinvent myself, but we've all been through a lot lately. Maybe a little rejuvenation is just what we need? Maybe I'll join you."

By the time dinner was over, they had all decided to attend the summit.

Their individual checks had come, and they had all thrown in their credit cards, when Madge noticed that Trish was quietly talking to the maître d' with a look of distress on her face. While the others were saying their goodbyes, Madge went over and Trish, red-faced, explained her credit card was denied. Madge immediately gave her card to the maître d', and told Trish not to worry, there was obviously some mistake with the credit card company.

7

MEAN GIRLS

Suzy had just arrived home when her cell phone rang. "Oh no, it's Hope," she said to Ken. "Do I dare even answer it?" She was tired and knew there was no such thing as a quick conversation with Hope. Ken knew she'd answer it and poured her a glass of wine, knowing she would need it.

"Oh Suzy, I'm so happy you answered the phone. I won't keep you long. But someone in our group has betrayed me!"

"Hope, what on earth are you talking about?"

"Well, did you get invited to Ellen's private party at 54 Below last week?"

"No, but then again I wouldn't have expected to be invited. I'm not really part of Ellen's crowd."

"Well, when I got home, my doorman handed me an envelope that he said had been dropped off at the door shortly after I left for our dinner. I opened it up and there was a photo of Ellen's party that was attended by several of our Ripe Tomatoes and other pals too. And the note said, 'We were all there and you weren't invited'," said a sobbing Hope into the phone.

"Oh, sweetie, that's terrible. Who would be that mean?"

"Well, I've never been so hurt in my entire life, and I will find out who did this." Hope then rattled off a half dozen suspects.

"Oh, Hope, I can't image any one of those women ever doing something like this. You need to let this go and remember all the wonderful friends you have who do love you."

"Well thanks, Suzy, but I am not letting this one go."

"Okay, sweetie, we'll talk later this week. Try to get some sleep."

Ken looked at Suzy. "What the heck was that all about?"

"Middle-aged mean girls," Suzy replied.

8

REVELATIONS

Trish headed up in the elevator to the twentieth floor. Fred, the elevator operator was his usual chatty self. "It's a beautiful summer night out there isn't it, Mrs. Hogan?" She barely heard him, and rushed out when the elevator doors opened to her floor. She entered the apartment and as always was swept away by the city views — Central Park to the north and the Freedom Tower to the south. It never grows old, she thought.

But tonight, she knew she had to confront Michael. Something was very wrong. Her black AMEX card had just been declined. And for weeks, Michael had been avoiding having dinner at the club, which used to be a weekly ritual. And while Michael quickly whisked the bills away, she had noticed several that said Final Notice. What on earth was happening?

She met Michael about two years after she moved from her native Chicago to New York City. He was a few years older, and already doing really well on Wall Street. A math wizard with a PhD from MIT, Michael was recruited by Goldman Sachs to be a quant analyst, developing complex mathematical models about risk management and investments.

While she was sharing a tiny one-bedroom apartment with Madge and Suzy and bringing home leftover food after client meetings at the agency, Michael had a beautiful, spacious two-bedroom apartment with a terrace on the East Side, a share in a house in the Hamptons, a great sports car, and a very generous expense account.

They got married a year later at the Metropolitan Club (which Michael had joined) and then spent two weeks in France and Italy for their honeymoon. When Trish found out she couldn't have children, they decided they would be each other's children. Everyone considered them one of the most devoted couples they knew.

Trish had been an art major in college, and shortly after she and Michael married, she left the ad agency world and went to work for a small art gallery in the West Village. She had found her passion and she was really quite good at spotting the next up-and-coming artist.

Michael eventually became a managing partner at Goldman Sachs, and ten years later, he and another colleague, David Brent, left to start their own hedge fund and were making obscene amounts of money.

It was Michael's idea that Trish should open her own gallery. She named it 40 Greenwich, which was the address of the gallery. She was known for her wonderful opening nights featuring new artists, and between her friends and Michael's clients, her artists were supported. The gallery itself just about broke even, but that was fine — it was never about the money. There was always plenty of it, and Michael took care of their finances so she could focus on art and making their life together wonderful.

She walked through the beautifully decorated living room, whose walls were adorned with some of her favorite artists, to the forty-foot-long terrace where Michael was smoking a cigar. As he rose to kiss her she said, "Michael, something very strange happened tonight. My AMEX card was declined."

"Trish, sit down." And then he said those dreaded words... "We need to talk."

***

Trish awakened to the smell of hot coffee from the mug Michael had placed on her nightstand. She could hear him shaving in the bathroom. She sat up and took a sip of coffee as she thought about last night's shocking revelation.

Michael told her that his hedge fund had been in trouble for over a year and was now experiencing double-digit losses. With returns

31

to investors dwindling, many of them had pulled out of the fund to the tune of one billion dollars. Michael and his partner, David, now had no choice except to shut down the fund and return seven billion dollars in capital to investors. With his hands over his face, Michael had sobbed when he apologized for failing her, and told her they would have no money coming in until he could figure out what to do next, and they would have no choice but to downsize considerably.

Her first reaction last night had been shock. Then she felt overwhelmingly sorry for Michael who clearly was feeling like a failure for the first time in his life. But this morning, she found herself feeling angry.

When Michael walked back into the bedroom she said, "How could you, Michael? How could you keep this from me for over a year? I'm your wife!"

Michael sat on the side of the bed. "I know, Trish, I know. I kept thinking things would get better. And you've never really taken much of an interest in the business side of things, and I just didn't want you to have to worry too."

"Oh, so in other words, 'Don't worry my pretty little head'," she hurled at him.

"For Christ's sake, Trish, that's not what I meant, and I don't need this now. We're making the announcement today. There will be a lot of fallout, and it will, of course, make the press. You need to be prepared. I have to leave. We'll talk tonight." And then he walked out the door.

Trish got out of bed, threw on a T-shirt, yoga pants, and sneakers, and headed out the door for a run through Central Park. She needed to clear her head.

9

TURMOIL

As soon as Madge got off the air, she rushed to her office and stared at the news feed on her phone again. She couldn't believe it. How could Trish not have mentioned this? And her card being declined at dinner was now starting to make sense.

She immediately called Suzy on her cell.

"Suzy, there's big news coming down today. Michael just announced he's shutting down his hedge fund and returning over seven billion dollars to investors."

She was stunned. "Wow, that's quite a shocker. Why didn't Trish say anything? And what will that mean for Trish and Michael personally?"

"I think it means they're going to be in one heck of a financial hole. We need to let Trish know we're here for her."

Suzy volunteered to reach out to Trish and see if she'd meet them for lunch over the weekend.

Madge hung up, thinking, *Well I guess I'm not the only one with problems these days.* She worried about Trish who always floated above problems and conflict with her eternal optimism. She'd need it.

Madge was wishing she had some of that optimism right about now. The rumors were rampant that with her contract coming up for renewal, she'd be moved to the noon spot with news and entertainment and Heather would step into her spot in the morning show. Just one step closer to fading her out. She needed some air, and threw on a pair of flats, grabbed her bag, and headed to the elevator.

Her go-to spot for de-stressing was Bryant Park, and she found a small table under the shade of a tree. Just as she sat down, her phone pinged. *I bet it's Suzy.* But to her utter surprise, it was a text from Jason Madison.

She had sent him a text right after the interview fiasco with Heather. She had simply said, "Sorry about the interview. I would never have violated your privacy." She hadn't expected a reply back, and now three weeks later, here was a text from Jason. "I'm the one who needs to apologize. Would you like to have dinner tonight?"

And as if her fingers had a mind of their own, she texted back, "Yes. What time and where?"

She sat back in her chair. *What the hell have I just done?*

***

Suzy had called and texted Trish several times. No response. Well, she'd have to deal with that later. The Arpello client was coming in today to review the latest round of creative for the repositioning brand launch. In addition to the client marketing people, the president of the fragrance division, Margot Tuttinger, would be there too.

Margot was truly a legend in the fragrance industry, so this was a big deal. Suzy would be presenting the research they'd done with millennial females, as the lead-up to the new positioning and presentation of the creative. She would, of course, present with enthusiasm, but her gut was still telling her they were off the mark and the real audience to reposition the brand to was women over forty-five.

Everyone was settled into the ergonomic chairs in the agency's high-tech conference room. After introductions, Suzy launched into the setup. "As we all know, Arpello was once the top brand in the world for young women with its innocent hints of first love, lust, and romance. But then they grew up and moved on to more sophisticated brands. Our research into today's young women shows that while they too love fragrances, they flaunt their sexuality and 'romance' is more about hookups on Tinder."

She dove a bit more into the research and set the stage nicely for Ryan to step in to present the new positioning and the creative concept, which focused around Tinder. The video spot featured a young woman in a midriff top and cutoff shorts that clung to her ample derriere, who was messaging a super hot guy on Tinder. When he asks, "What are you wearing?" she says, "Nothing but Arpello,"and the music is one of those sexually explicit, fuck-me-now songs.

The Arpello marketing team loved it. Margot Tuttinger showed no emotion at all during the presentation, not surprising since that's her trademark. Ryan was ecstatic by the enthusiasm of the marketing team. At the end of the meeting, he invited the client and agency teams to meet at Buddakan for drinks and dinner.

Suzy politely bowed out saying she had a Friday night family commitment. Margot also bowed out. "I'm going to head home. I have a flight to Paris tomorrow."

Well, that's that, thought Suzy as she walked back to her office to grab her things. *I guess Ryan was right*, she sighed and headed to the elevator.

The door was just about to close when she heard Margot's distinctive voice, "Would you mind holding that?"

10

FIRST DATE

Madge felt like a high school girl on her first date. But was this even a date? Really, how ridiculous of her to think that. She was fourteen years older than Jason and he had *Sports Illustrated* swimwear models chasing after him. His text when she replied yes, said, "The loft, 8:00 p.m. An apology dinner for my rude behavior last time we met." Clearly, he was just being polite.

She decided to dress casually. A summer shift and flat sandals, and her hair casually swept up with a clip. Without her usual on-camera makeup and anchor hairdo, she actually looked younger. *Well, here goes.* She rang the buzzer and the door clicked open. She took the elevator to the second floor. And there was Jason. Dressed in a black pair of jeans with a white shirt, collar opened, and sleeves rolled up, he looked sexy as hell with that wonderful smile. The office area was empty now.

"Wow, look at you," he said appreciatively. "I like the casual Madge, girl reporter. I thought we'd eat in, and I love to cook. Do you mind? We can head upstairs to my space."

"You cook too?" said Madge. "I love eating in, although in my case it's always food I've ordered in."

They headed two flights up the spiral staircase, into a beautiful open loft area, with floor-to-ceiling windows, and a fabulous outdoor terrace with amazing city views.

"White or red?" While he opened the wine, Madge gazed around the very comfortably decorated space. Big oversize couches, a sixty-inch flat screen display, a huge fireplace, and a spacious open kitchen area with a large center island and comfy bar stools. There was another spiral staircase to another loft area that she assumed was where he slept. A very comfortable man cave.

With wine in hand, they headed out to the terrace where Jason had put out a tray of snacks.

"Thanks for coming tonight, Madge. I really did behave badly when we met last time, and I understand why you decided not to be the one to interview me."

Madge practically choked on her wine.

"Ahh...well...Jason, it wasn't my decision not to do the interview. It was the network's decision. They thought Heather interviewing you would appeal more to a younger generation."

"That's insane. She can't hold a candle to you as an interviewer."

"Well thanks, Jason, but it's a tough business I'm in, especially as a woman. When we hit a certain age, our opportunities start to diminish." And before Madge knew it, she was opening up to Jason about her career problems. He was really listening, and asking excellent questions too.

Over dinner, a delicious pasta dish with fresh vegetables from the farmer's market in Union Square, that Jason whipped up effortlessly, their conversation flowed from one topic to another — current events, work, and life.

"If you could be doing anything you wanted to do career-wise," Jason asked, "what would it be?" They had moved over to a very comfortable couch on the terrace and Jason had brought out an aged bottle of port.

"You mean, what do I want to be when I grow up? I'd still like to be 'Madge, Girl Reporter', but I'd like to be doing stories that make a difference. That can inspire, and maybe change how people think. I'm sick of the mostly bad news that's fed to viewers today in two-minute segments. I think they're smarter than that."

"Well, why don't you just do it?"

Madge laughed. "When I make my first billion dollars, I'll start my own network."

They talked some more, when Madge looked at her watch. "I need to get going. I didn't realize it was so late. I've definitely overstayed my welcome."

Jason gave her a long gaze with those beautiful eyes and said, "You're always welcome," and before she could protest (right, like she would have), he leaned in and locked her in an embrace with one of the longest and best kisses she could recall.

Madge reluctantly pulled away.

"Madge, this was one of the nicest evenings I've spent with anyone in a long, long time. Thank you."

He walked her downstairs where he insisted on calling an Uber for her, gently kissed her on the cheek, and opened the car door for her.

I'm in trouble now, Madge sighed to herself.

11

SPILLING THE BEANS

Ken was making the martinis as Suzy walked in the door. "You said to have a drink ready, and here it is."

Suzy gratefully took the martini, kicked off her shoes, and plopped herself on the couch. "Thank you, sweetheart, I needed this. What a day."

Ken joined her. "Well, it was certainly all over the financial news about Michael closing down the hedge fund. That's all anyone at the firm could talk about. I had heard rumors, but I had no idea things had gotten this bad. Have you talked to Trish?"

"I've left her several messages, but she hasn't responded. I'm worried about her. Madge and I were hoping to get her out to lunch this weekend and find out how she is."

"Well, I'm sure this has been a hellava day for both of them. She's probably just hiding out. I'm sure she'll call. So how was the big pitch today?"

Suzy loved that Ken was such a great sounding board for her. He always asked about her day first, even though he was a big deal corporate attorney and had tough days too. In fact, she realized some days she was so wrapped up in her day, she forgot to ask about his.

"Ken, you are not going to believe what happened. The client's twelve-year-old marketing team was there, but the president was there too. You've heard me talk about her — Margot Tuttinger — she's a legend. Well, the twelve-year-olds loved the creative concept. Ryan was ecstatic and gave me that little 'see I told you so' smirk. The kids were going to celebrate over dinner and probably tequila shots later in the evening, which I declined as did Margot. We ended up heading down the elevator together and she asked me to join her for a cup of tea.

"So, get this. We exchanged pleasantries, our tea arrived, and then she asked me, point-blank, what did I really think about the repositioning of the brand. I danced around a bit, said the research shows that millennial women love fragrances, and the creative approach tapped into today's dating hookup scene.

"But Margot pushed and asked with her piercing eyes and no-nonsense tone of voice, 'But what do *you* really think? I sensed there was something more when you talked so passionately about the generation of women who loved Arpello when they were young?'

"So, I blurted out my idea about this being a retro brand that could be repositioned to women my age, who I think would fall in love with the brand all over again."

"And what did she say?" asked Ken.

"She said, 'Thank you for your candor, Suzy'. And then she paid the check and told me to enjoy the evening."

***

On Saturday morning, Trish finally responded to Suzy's texts, and agreed to meet for brunch on Sunday at Fiorello's. They usually liked to sit outside to people watch around Lincoln Center, but Suzy figured this could get a little emotional today and asked for a quiet table inside in the back. She knew she had made the right decision when Trish walked in wearing her sunglasses and didn't take them off until their Bloody Marys arrived. You could tell she hadn't been sleeping and obviously had been crying a lot.

Madge gently put her hand on Trish's and said, "Sweetie, why didn't you tell us what was going on?"

Her answer stunned Suzy and Madge.

"Michael never said a word to you?" said Suzy.

"No. And now I feel like a fool for not knowing what was going on. You know I've never been good with money. Remember when we were young and my checking account got out of control because I couldn't balance my checkbook? I'd just close it down and open another account. And I admit, when Michael would try to talk to me about finances, stocks, and investments, my eyes would glaze over. So, I just let him handle everything.

"I was shocked when he told me. And then I got really, really angry about it. And I'm still angry, but if you could just see him. He looks so beaten down. I've never seen him like this. And that's when I realized that I need to be on his team, not against him, to get us through this."

Suzy and Madge didn't interrupt, because they knew Trish needed to get this all out.

"But honestly, I'm not even sure where to begin. I told Michael we'll put the Hamptons house on the market right away. And we don't need two luxury leased cars in the city. In fact, we don't even need a car. And I'd give up the gallery, but the lease is paid for a year. Although I can't support any more shows there. So that's it...we're going to have to figure this out as we go along."

"Well, you know we're here for you, and if you need any money," Madge started to say and then Trish cut her off.

"No, we'll be fine. Your emotional support and being here is all I need. So enough about my soap-opera life, what's happening with you two?"

Suzy told them about her encounter with Margot Tuttinger. "Now I'm thinking it was such a stupid thing to do. If Ryan ever finds out, I'll be canned."

Trish, who even in her own distress can always sense others' emotions, looked at Madge and said, "You're very quiet today. What's going on with you?"

"Well, there's all the network crap. And I'm fairly certain I'll get moved to the midday news desk, which really sucks."

"And what else...?" Trish probed.

"Okay, okay, okay. I had a date. Sort of."

"Who with?" asked Suzy, "And was it another online dating fiasco?"

"Actually I didn't meet him online. And it definitely wasn't a fiasco. It fact, it was a great evening and ended with one of the best kisses I've ever had. But I can't see him again."

"What??" Trish and Suzy shouted in unison. "Spill the beans."

"I had dinner with Jason Madison at his loft. He even cooked dinner. But he's only thirty-eight years old. A kid really. I'm sure it was the wine. He has twenty-year-old models chasing after him. I wouldn't even be able to take my clothes off in front of him. But he did give me some good career advice to think about."

"Well, you know what," said Suzy, "it's great timing that we're all going to that rejuvenation convention in a few weeks. Sounds like just the thing we need."

12

JUMPING OFF THE CLIFF

"I quit."

It was noon on Thursday, two weeks before Labor Day, and with those two simple words, Madge walked away from a twenty-five-year career at the network. She had agonized all week. On Monday, the network presented her with a new contract that not only moved her to the midday news and entertainment hour, but also cut her to one interview a month on *That's All, Folks* and reduced her salary by 20 percent!

Jack, of course, tried to position it as a great opportunity for her. "We know you'll bring the ratings up in this time slot, which will get us more advertising dollars. And we've added a bonus incentive tied to ratings points that could double your salary. And of course, you'll still have a monthly interview on Sunday nights."

All week long she had weighed the pros and cons. She had grown up at the network, and in many ways, it felt like family. She had loved the glamour and the excitement. She had traveled the world and met amazing people. But she had to admit she was getting tired, and bored too. The business was more competitive than ever. The morning news had turned into entertainment, with cooking segments, interviews with spoiled celebrities, and every season she felt they did the same old segments — holiday tips for looking great this season, how to make your own wrapping paper (ridiculous), and other inane topics. And when they did get a chance to interview someone on a meaningful topic, it was a five-minute segment.

And then there was the quest for the fountain of youth. She had to constantly work out and diet to stay at least ten pounds below her ideal weight because the camera adds pounds. And from the time she was thirty-five she had turned to Botox, wrinkle fillers, and weekly facials to keep the signs of aging from showing. Every time she looked in the mirror these days she realized she was losing that battle and the next step would be a facelift. But did she really want to look like all those other plastic mannequins that were churned out daily by New York City's top plastic surgeons?

She had to admit, Jason's words kept coming back to her too. *What do you really want to do, Madge? And why are you doing something you're not enjoying anymore?*

She couldn't stop thinking about Jason even though she was avoiding him. He had texted her several times about having dinner again, and she had simply replied, "Sorry, up to my eyeballs in work."

And now, here she was in her apartment in the middle of the afternoon with the rest of her life ahead of her and no idea what to do with it.

Oh my God, what have I done? she thought, as she stood looking out the floor-to-ceiling windows of her living room, barely noticing the breathtaking views of the East River and Lower Manhattan. She had bought this two-bedroom Murray Hill condo on the forty-eighth floor not long after she started making her first real money as an on-air newscaster during the 1990s real estate downturn. And now it was worth a pretty penny. She threw on a pair of old sweatpants, turned her phone off, and went to raid her fridge. "Pathetic," she thought. "Well, Prosecco and a box of dark chocolates will have to do."

She brought the bottle and the chocolates into the living room, flipped on the TV to Turner Classic Movies and started watching the original *Sunset Boulevard* with Gloria Swanson. Perfect for the mood she was in — a fading star and a fading news anchor.

***

"Madge, Madge, wake up."

Madge slowly opened her eyes to see Suzy and Trish standing in her living room where she had fallen asleep on the couch after finishing off the Prosecco and watching old movies most of the night. They both had keys to her apartment in case of an emergency. She guessed this constituted an emergency.

"We've been so worried about you," Trish said. "You're on Page Six of the *Post* this morning, which is how we found out what happened. And you weren't answering your phone."

"I'm sorry. I just wasn't up to talking to anyone, not even my two best friends."

"Well, I see you had your other two best friends with you," laughed Suzy as she picked up the empty bottle and chocolate wrappings off the floor.

"Can you make us some coffee, Suzy, while I take a quick shower?"

Ten minutes later they were all settled in Madge's living room.

Madge walked them through her agonizing week of going back and forth on whether to accept the contract or just leave.

"And you know when I walked into Jack's office yesterday morning, I still wasn't sure what I was going to do. But once he started saying how I could save the day for midday in that damned condescending way of his, I knew I just couldn't do it anymore. He was basically offering me the shit end of a stick and coating it with honey."

"Well, I think that's just about the bravest thing you've ever done, Madge," said Suzy. "You've been unhappy for a long time. I wish I had some of your courage."

"Well, it felt really good in the moment to say, 'I quit', but I have to say I'm really not feeling that brave this morning. And Trish, what was that you said about me being in Page Six?"

"Oh, it was nothing, really," said Trish. "Just a little mention that you've left the network."

"Trish, you could never tell a lie. What exactly was the little mention?"

"Okay, you'd eventually see it anyway." Trish pulled the paper out of her tote bag and reluctantly handed it to Madge.

The headline was "*Good Morning New York* Replaces Madge Thompson with Sexy Heather Stone".

Madge read out loud, "The *Good Morning New York* show announced today that thirty-year-old Heather Stone would be taking over from fifty-two-year-old Madge Thompson. Rumors have been swirling for some time that the network is trying to build a following with the prized twenty-four to thirty-five year old demographic and didn't feel it could do that with its aging anchor."

"Christ! When did fifty-two become old? Should I just head out on the iceberg now?"

"And you two wondered why I didn't want a big celebration for my fiftieth birthday," said Suzy. "But I have figured out how I want to celebrate with my two best friends. I've booked us into a very exclusive spa in Vermont for the next three days. And we certainly all need a getaway right now. So, you each have two hours to pack a bag. This is Ken's treat for the three of us, and he has his firm's private plane waiting for us at Teterboro to fly us to Manchester. We'll be there in time for cocktails."

13

THE SPA

They agreed on the plane ride that they were leaving their problems behind for a couple of days and weren't going to discuss their muddled lives. The drive from the Manchester airport was beautiful. Surrounded by the majestic green beauty of Vermont's mountains, they were starting to feel less stressed already. They passed through the charming town of Manchester and then headed up a long and winding mountain road. When they reached the top there was the beautiful post and beam spa, surrounded by mountains.

They walked into the spacious and comfortably furnished reception and living room area. The beamed ceilings and large windows that captured the vista made the room even more spacious. One wall was a floor-to-ceiling stone fireplace. At the other end were French doors that led out to a very large deck with rocking chairs. A perfect getaway, or so it seemed.

The spa manager made her way over to welcome them. At the same time, a group of women came in through the French doors, dressed in khakis, wearing hiking boots, and carrying backpacks. They all glanced in the direction of the new arrivals who screamed New York City. Madge was wearing a pair of skinny jeans and four-inch-high Manolos. Trish was in her Lululemon yoga gear from head to toe. Suzy was wearing Chanel black capri pants, a white boyfriend shirt, and Prada flats.

"Welcome to the Green Mountain Lodge and Spa. I'm Kimmy and I'm here to make your visit tranquil, healthy, and restorative. And which one of you is Mrs. Hamilton?"

"That would be me," replied Suzy, "and my friends and I are looking forward to our visit. I understand you have a three-bedroom cabin reserved for us."

"Yes, follow me this way."

Kimmy led them along a winding path that brought them to a secluded cabin, with great views, and its own deck as well. The cabin was also post and beam and furnished with large overstuffed couches, and cozy chairs facing another beautiful stone fireplace. The bedrooms were large, each had a fireplace, and all led out onto the deck. Madge was starting to feel better already.

After they had deposited their belongings in their rooms, they met Kimmy back in the living room for an overview of the resort and the various activities. There was a lake about a quarter-mile walk where they could swim or kayak. There was an extensive spa services menu, including hot rock massages and mud scrubs. "And I highly recommend the colonics and digestive release massages," perky Kimmy added.

There were hiking adventures, birding expeditions, meditation, and yoga classes. Dinner was served from 6:00 to 7:30 p.m. in the main dining room, breakfast from 6:00 to 7:30 a.m., lunch from noon to 2:00 p.m. And every afternoon at 4:00 p.m. tea was served on the main deck.

"Any questions?" asked the now annoyingly perky Kimmy.

"Yes, I have a couple of questions," said Madge. "Where are the TVs and where is the bar?"

"Oh, we don't have TVs on the property. We find it interferes with the tranquility of the experience. We encourage our guests to read in the evenings, or just spend quiet time surrounded by nature. And we don't serve or permit alcohol on the premises. Feel free to explore the grounds before dinner. And by the way, we do have a shop that sells hiking shoes and other outdoor attire in case you traveled here light," Kimmy said diplomatically while eyeing Madge's stilettos. "Oh, and there's no cell service up here, but we do have landlines in all the rooms." And with that bit of breaking news, perky Kimmy headed back to the main lodge.

Suzy was the first to speak. "Well, I admit I didn't know they were a no-alcohol spa, but let's look at this as a good time to give our livers a little break."

"I agree," said Trish, "and reading myself to sleep sounds like a luxury."

"Well, this will be an interesting adventure. I don't think I'll be trying the 'digestive relief massage', sounds a little scary. But I'm actually glad that no one can reach me on my cell. And at least we can go shopping," said Madge. "Come on, we need hiking shoes."

***

"The last time I ate dinner at 6:00 p.m., I was seven years old, but I'm starving," said Madge, as the trio made their way to the dining room.

"Would you like hot water and lemon, green tea — hot or cold — or water from our very own mountain stream?" asked their server, Tammy, who must have gone to perky school with Kimmy.

"Well, I'd prefer a vodka martini, but your mountain water will do," said Madge.

Trish ordered the hot water with lemon. "It's wonderful for the digestive system." And Suzy ordered an iced green tea.

Tammy came back with their drinks and a basket of gluten-free rolls and vegan butter.

"Our menu consists of delicious small portions and each meal is under four hundred calories," Tammy proudly pronounced. "The vegetables are all grown in our organic garden."

They opened the menus where the three dinner choices were revealed. Choice #1, sautéed rapini with a baked whipped sweet potato; Choice #2, kale salad with hemp seeds, organic baby carrots, and fennel; Choice #3, broccoli walnut salad. And the choice of parsnip soup or bone broth with each entrée.

"I just love all these wonderful healthy choices," said Trish with her usual enthusiasm for all things healthy. "We should order one of each and share."

While their dinners were being plucked from the garden, they reviewed the activities list for the following day. After much discussion they agreed to start the day off with a meditation session (Trish's suggestion of course), followed by breakfast (Madge's suggestion), the guided nature hike, followed by a swim in the lake (Suzy's suggestion).

"After breathing in car fumes and unidentified subway smells, our lungs won't know what to do with all this fresh air," said Suzy.

"Thanks, Suzy," said Madge. "I mean really, thanks. I know I arrived acting like the typical New York City snob in the country with the hicks, but I think this is just what we all needed, and I am so happy to spend quality time with the two of you."

And with that dinner arrived. Although dinner would be an overstatement. Their meals were served on small plates and the portions were barely enough for one person, never mind for sharing. They dug in ravenously and five minutes later dinner was complete.

Perky Tammy was making the dessert rounds, and announced, "Our dessert tonight is carrot flan and quinoa pilaf. Can I interest you ladies?

They said yes in unison, and then Madge added, "And I'd like an espresso too."

"Oh, I'm so sorry, we don't serve coffee or anything with caffeine. Our after-dinner beverage choices are a caffeine-free hemp tea for relaxation, or a fermented tea that's wonderful for digestion."

***

"Well, here we are back at the ranch," said Suzy kicking off her shoes. "At least the two-inch square flan was tasty, unlike the rest of the meal."

"And it's just too bad they took the good stuff out of the hemp tea," added Madge. "So, here we are, ladies. It's 8:00 p.m. What do we do for entertainment?"

"I know," said Trish, "let's play Have You Ever."

"I'm in," said Suzy.

"Me too," said Madge, "but you know when it comes to 'have you ever' I have never said never!"

They chuckled at the truth of that, made a roaring fire, and amused themselves for the next hour or so.

"Okay, ladies," said Suzy, "We have a big day tomorrow, which starts at 6:00 a.m. for meditation. I'm off to sleep."

"Me too," said Trish, never a night owl.

"Listen," said Madge, "before we turn in, thanks for coming to the rescue this morning. I don't know what I would do without the two of you." They all hugged and headed to their rooms, laughingly shouting out "goodnight moon", "goodnight stars", "goodnight besties."

***

Suzy and Trish were out on the deck when a very groggy Madge appeared. "God, I would do just about anything for a cup of coffee. I had the worst night's sleep."

"You did?" said Trish incredulously. "Well, I slept like a baby and woke up to the sound of mourning doves."

"Sleep? How could you sleep with all that racket from the crickets? I need sirens and honking horns to lull me to sleep," laughed Madge.

"Well, I'd love coffee too, but since that's not happening, let's hope the meditation takes the edge off," said Suzy. "Let's go, ladies."

Madge couldn't help peeking around the room at everyone in their lotus positions. She had never been able to meditate, and this morning was no different. Her mind was in a whirl reviewing events of the past few days and her butt was getting sore. When the thirty minutes ended it had seemed like an eternity.

"Wasn't that wonderfully relaxing? A perfect way to start the day," said Trish as they headed to the main lodge for breakfast — hot lemon water, fruit, and a free-range poached egg on quinoa. After breakfast they strolled to the lake to meet their hiking guide.

For the next two hours they followed "Brunhilda" on the not-so-gentle climb up what was advertised as the beginner's hike to reach the summit of Mount Derby.

"Look at this glorious view," said Trish, who practically skipped all the way up the trail, happily taking in the summit panorama.

Suzy and Madge were just happy to finally sit down. Glorious was not quite how they'd describe the blisters on their feet from the three-hundred-dollar hiking shoes they hadn't broken in, bug bites, and twig scratches. Not to mention they still had to get back down.

"Well," said Suzy, "Let's think about that refreshing swim in the lake."

***

"Last one in's a rotten egg," shouted Suzy as she flew down the hill toward the lake.

Madge and Trish had just crested the top of the hill when they heard Suzy shouting, "Holy shit. Did someone throw ice cubes in the lake?" She hurried out and wrapped herself in a towel.

Madge and Trish stuck their toes in the water and immediately recoiled too. "Well, so much for the lake swim. Let's head to the spa for massages," said Suzy.

By 4:00 p.m., they were sitting in the rocking chairs on the main deck, each with a cup of tea. "Well, the hot rock massage was delightful, and my sore muscles and blistered feet are much better," a more relaxed Madge said. "Now if I just had a martini and a hamburger to look forward to, I'd be in Heaven."

"I wish you hadn't said that. Now I'm salivating for a burger and a martini would be delightful," agreed Suzy.

"Well," said Trish. "It's not like we're prisoners here. Maybe we can go into town tonight for dinner."

"Well, we're not prisoners," said Suzy, "but the spa definitely frowns on guests breaking with protocol. In fact, their materials say if you can't commit to the first forty-eight-hour regimen, they'd prefer you just leave so as not to disrupt the yin and yang of the spa experience. And if we don't show up for dinner, that will be a problem."

They rocked in silence for a few more minutes, when Madge said, "I've got it. I know how we can escape."

14

THE ESCAPE

By 7:30 p.m. they were halfway down the mountain access road where Madge had told the cab driver to pick them up. They had told the spa they were too exhausted to eat in the dining room and had ordered their meals delivered to the cabin. And when they lifted the lids on the evening's fare, they knew heading into town was the right decision.

They jumped in the cab, changed out of their hiking boots, and asked the cabbie to take them to the best restaurant in town. They were like giddy teenagers who'd just escaped from their bedroom window.

"Well, the Homestead's a real popular local place. Good burgers, steaks, and music too," said the cabbie. "You girls from New York City?"

"Well, yes we are."

"That's what I thought. It's always the New York City gals who call for the cabs and the pickup halfway down the road," he said chuckling.

A half hour later, they were settled at the rustic bar while they waited for a table, and taking their first sips of the Moose Martini the bartender had suggested. The place was hopping.

"Well, here's to us, the three tomatoes," said Suzy. "I haven't had this much guilty fun since Catholic school when we'd sneak cigarettes in the bathroom."

They clinked glasses, when suddenly Madge gasped!

"What's wrong?" a worried Suzy asked.

"Oh my God...Jason just walked in and he's with a beautiful, tall, twentysomething blonde. I need to hide."

"It's too late," said Suzy, "he's heading this way."

And then there he was. With that gorgeous smile and beautiful eyes. Madge was feeling more than a pang of jealousy of his beautiful young date.

"Madge, what are you doing here? I've been texting you for two days. This is the last place I ever expected to see you."

"Well, I didn't expect to see you either. What are you doing here?"

"I live here."

"Oh right. Ahh...let me introduce my partners-in-crime – my best friends, Suzy and Trish. We've just escaped from the loony bin spa on top of the mountain for martinis and burgers," Madge explained hurriedly, hoping he'd quickly return to his date.

Jason laughed that wonderful laugh of his. "Yes, I've heard they're a bit extreme. It's nice to meet you both. Hey, would you like to join us for dinner? I have a table reserved in the back."

"Oh no, we wouldn't want to disturb you and your date. And we'd need more than a cozy table for two."

"My date?" said Jason quizzically. "Oh, you mean my sister, Chrissy. She runs my horse farm. I'd love you to meet her. And I know the owner so I'm sure we can get a bigger table."

Chrissy was adorable and smart too. Horses were not only her passion, but her business, and apparently, she was one of the best horse trainers in New England. Jason had ordered a wonderful bottle of wine, and the burgers did not disappoint, nor did the conversation. Jason and Chrissy talked about their love of Vermont, and Jason said it was the place that kept him grounded. "I wish you were all staying here longer, so we could give you a tour of the farm," said Jason. "You'll just have to come up again," he said to the group, but he was looking straight at Madge.

Shortly after nine, a jazz trio showed up. Madge had expected a country group, so she was pleasantly surprised as they started playing classic tunes from *The American Songbook*.

65

Suzy and Trish couldn't help but notice that Jason never took his eyes off Madge for more than a moment. When the trio started playing *"Unforgettable,"* Jason stood up and put his hand out to Madge. "Come, let's dance."

He held her close, and Madge was getting dizzy breathing in his musky smell.

"So, what does it feel like to be a free woman, Madge?"

"Truthfully? I feel like I'm free-falling off a cliff. It's scary as hell."

"You did the right thing, Madge, and I'll be here to catch you," he whispered in her ear as he held her a little tighter.

The song ended way too soon, and they headed back to the table.

"Well, as difficult as it is to leave this wonderful evening, we do have to sneak back into the spa," said Suzy. "I called our friendly conspirator cabby. He'll be here in ten minutes."

They said their goodbyes. And Jason pulled Madge to the side. "Listen, I'll be back in the city on Wednesday, and no more excuses about dinner. I'll pick you up at 8:00 p.m." Madge nodded in agreement.

They were back in the cab, hiking boots back on as the cabbie made his way up the mountain road.

"I have a little treat for us," said Trish. "I had the bartender make us three Moose Martinis to go."

"Trish, you never cease to amaze us," said Suzy.

The cabbie wanted to drive them to the door, but they insisted they'd be okay using their iPhones as flashlights to get back to the lodge, undetected.

They approached the lodge and made their way to the path on the left that led to their cabin. Except fifteen minutes later they were still trying to find their cabin.

"Oh no, I think we're lost," said Madge, "and I have to pee really badly."

"Shhh...not so loud," said Suzy, but then she started giggling. "I can't believe we actually escaped." And then her giggle turned into full-on laughter, and before they knew what hit them, they were all laughing hysterically.

"Oh, we're here," said Trish, tears from the laughter running down her cheeks as they finally turned the corner to their cabin, where she abruptly stopped laughing.

Standing at their doorway was Kimmy, the spa manager, and she definitely did not look perky.

Inside the cabin, a very stern Kimmy informed them that they were no longer welcome at the inn, and would have to pack their bags and leave first thing in the morning. "We expect our guests to take the spa rules seriously," chided Kimmy, in a tone that would have made Sister Mary Joseph proud. The second she left, they broke into gales of laughter again and finished the Moose Martinis.

15

THE FARM

"Well, we've got a bit of a problem," said Suzy. They were having breakfast in town, with their first real coffee in two days. What could be wrong?

"Ken said the company plane can't pick us up until tomorrow morning, as scheduled, and all the inns and B&Bs in the area are booked. The only car rental place says there won't be any cars available at the airport until *maybe* late tonight and the trains are booked. We're screwed."

They drank their coffee in silence.

"Well, I have a thought," said Madge. "I could call Jason and see if he can give us the tour of the farm today and maybe he has room to put us up? I'll tell him we don't mind sleeping on couches."

One little phone call and an hour later they were sitting on the veranda of Jason's beautiful eighteenth-century farmhouse sipping ice teas.

"Well, I guess we didn't have to worry about sleeping on couches. The guest rooms are just beautiful," laughed Madge.

When they arrived, Jason had led them to the second floor of the house where there were six beautiful guest rooms to choose from.

"Tell us about the house, Jason," said Suzy.

"This was my grandparents' farmhouse and I have great memories of spending my summer and school vacations here. After they died, the farm had a couple of different owners and had really fallen into disrepair. When it came on the market six years ago, I snatched it up. We've been restoring it ever since, but it's close to finished," Jason said proudly. "I'll give you a tour of the house before lunch, and then we can visit Chrissy's horses."

The furnishings were beautiful, with a combination of antiques and yard sale finds that had been lovingly refurbished. The old wooden floors had been restored and were adorned with Cape Cod hooked rugs. And they all loved the bright color paints and vibrant prints — yellows, reds, blues that made each room pop.

The first floor had a very large living room, which Jason explained had been three tiny rooms that he opened up. The living room led to an elegant dining room and that led to a wonderful country kitchen and great room.

"Ladies, meet Bertha. She's making us a dinner with vegetables from the garden and fresh eggs from the chicken coop."

Bertha had long braids and a very suntanned, weathered face. She was a big woman of indeterminate age and a warm welcoming smile. "I hope you ladies like ratatouille, egg casseroles, and homemade bread."

They all nodded with enthusiastic yeses.

The rest of the first floor had a library with a number of first edition classics that Jason had collected, and a comfortable study that was Jason's office.

The second floor had the guest rooms. Each room was intimate and comfortable, and three of them had their own bathrooms.

The third floor was smaller, and this was Jason's domain. He had an enormous master bedroom with a king-size canopy bed, a lovely sitting area, fireplace, and a balcony with a beautiful view of the land, the mountains, the farm, and the horses.

They spent the rest of the afternoon walking the property with its beautiful flower and vegetable gardens, the apple orchard, and the pond stocked with fish. Jason pointed out the barn that had been restored, and upstairs was Chrissy's apartment.

The best part of the day though was Chrissy's tour of the horse paddocks, meeting her beautiful horses, and watching them gallop in the fields. Chrissy offered to take them horseback riding, but since none of them had ever been on a horse, they politely declined.

Bertha had left dinner warming on the stove, and they all pitched in to set the table and put the food out. Jason opened some wine and they all settled into seats in the inviting kitchen.

Suzy raised her wineglass to toast Jason. "Well, here's to our knight in shining armor. You saved us from Brunhilda and that god-awful place they call a spa."

"I love saving damsels in distress," laughed Jason, looking at Madge. They clinked glasses all around.

Jason wanted to know more about each of them, and he was such a great listener they found themselves telling him more than they usually would with people they've only just met.

Suzy talked about her frustrations at the agency and the elevator run-in with Margot Tuttinger.

"Aunt Margot?" said Chrissy.

"On my gosh, I've really spoken out of school. She's related to you?" said a very chagrined Suzy.

"She was our mother's roommate at Wellesley," explained Jason. "We've known her all our lives, so she's sort of been an adopted aunt. In fact, she was the brand manager of Arpello in her early career and talked my father into being the Arpello man. And don't worry, we would never say a word. She's a tough nut, Suzy, but she likes smart people, and you are definitely that."

"Oh my gosh, that explains the resemblance," said Trish. "We told Suzy if she repositioned the brand you should be the model because you look like the original guy we all had crushes on." As soon as she said that, she blushed.

Jason just laughed, and said, "I'm not the model type and my dad did it reluctantly. So, tell me about your art gallery, Trish."

Trish told him about her gallery and that she'd like to figure out something to do with the space that would actually make money.

They got around to Madge. "Well, I honestly have no idea what my next thing will be, but I'm a whole lot less scared about the future than I was when this weekend adventure started. I mean, if we could escape the spa from hell, I think we can do anything."

They all clinked glasses on that, and then pitched in and cleaned up the kitchen.

It was only ten o'clock but it had been a long day and since they had to be at the airport by 7:00 a.m., they all agreed it was time to turn in. Jason had volunteered to drive them to the airport.

"Help yourself to coffee, tea, and whatever's in the fridge in the morning," said Jason. "We need to leave here at six. I'll meet you in the kitchen."

They thanked Jason and Chrissy for a wonderful day and delicious dinner and headed up to their rooms on the second floor.

Madge loved the room she was in with its own private bath. The bed was covered in a lovely hand-stitched quilt, and the beautiful old mahogany dresser with the old-fashioned pitcher and bowl was just right. The wallpaper was a delicate rose pattern. She took a long hot shower and as she soaped up she couldn't help thinking of Jason. Enough. She cut her shower short, changed into her silk PJs and climbed into the bed that felt like she was floating on a cloud. She knew she had to get to sleep, but for the next hour she simply tossed and turned. She couldn't get Jason out of her head.

I wonder if he's still awake? she thought. *Maybe we could just talk. And I'll explain to him why it makes no sense for us to be together.*

She got out of bed and gently opened the door a crack. No one in the hall, and the lights were out in Trish's and Suzy's rooms. She gently tiptoed up to the third floor and saw a light under Jason's closed door. She quietly made her way to the end of the hall, and lightly tapped. No answer. "Oh God, what am I doing here," she thought and was just about to turn away, when the door opened. There was Jason, bare-chested and wearing boxer shorts. He opened his arms and said, "What took you so long?"

Later as they lay in the moonlight, Jason said, "You're so beautiful," as he caressed her body after the hottest sex she had ever had, followed by the most loving sex she had ever had. The moon was shining in on this perfect boy/man and Madge felt a tenderness she'd never quite felt for any man before.

"You've got to stop with this age thing, Madge. I know it's a cliché, but it is just a number. You're beautiful, you're smart, you're fun, and you're brave. There's not a supermodel or fawning actress out there who could come anywhere near you. You need to believe that."

And in that moment, Madge did believe. She stayed enveloped in Jason's arms for a while longer, and then gently said, "Jason, I have to slip back to my room before Trish and Suzy get up. I don't want them to know about us yet."

He gave her another deep long kiss, and said, "I think they already suspect." And with that Madge headed back to her room, just in time to get dressed to head to the airport.

Jason walked to the tarmac with them to the private jet and hugged Suzy and Trish goodbye. He stood looking at Madge, moved toward her, and then gave her a gentle kiss on the cheek.

As soon as the plane was in the air, Suzy said, "You did the deed, didn't you?"

"Is it that obvious?"

"Yes," Trish and Suzy said in unison. "You're glowing."

16

THE END OF SUMMER

The week before Labor Day was slow at the office and the city was practically empty. Suzy picked up the phone and called Hope. They were long overdue for a lunch date.

"Hope, it's Suzy. I know it's short notice, but are you free for lunch today? I bet we can get into the Pool, and I haven't been there since they took over the space from the Four Seasons." Hope immediately agreed.

Suzy made a quick call, and as she suspected got a 1:00 p.m. lunch reservation at the city's hottest new "see and be seen" restaurant. Hope loved these kinds of places.

"Well, this is beautiful," said Hope looking around, and Suzy agreed. "So, what's been going on? How is Trish and what will Madge do next?"

Suzy was careful to give the public version — Trish will be fine, and Madge is excited about exploring new opportunities. She had Hope laughing hysterically about their spa adventure (leaving out any mention of Jason and the farm.) She loved Hope dearly, and knew she truly cared for her friends and always wanted to help, but she didn't trust that Hope would keep that kind of juicy gossip to herself.

"So, what's going on with you, Hope?"

"Well, I got another ugly note, similar to the last one. One of those, 'we all were invited and you weren't.' Honestly, it's so distressing. I really need to find out who's doing this to me."

"God, that really is just awful. I can't imagine who would do this." Then deliberately changing the subject because she knew Hope was ready to go into her conspiracy theories about who was out to get her, she asked, "So, how is it going with the play you've been trying to get financed?"

"Well, I've decided to postpone that particular play because I have one much more exciting in the hopper right now," Hope revealed.

"Can you tell me about it?"

Hope paused, and then said, "All right, but this is super confidential. I convinced Celeste that her story about her ninety-two-year-old billionaire boyfriend would make a fabulous musical. She's working on the story with a scriptwriter, and I have a brilliant songwriter working on the score. It's titled *If Tomorrow Never Comes*."

"That is so exciting. And how great that you and Celeste get to collaborate. My lips are sealed, of course," Suzy added. "And speaking of boyfriends, are you still dating the same guy?"

"Yes, Marvin has been a doll. He listens to me stress over this new show and thank goodness he was there when I got the last horrible note. I just collapsed in his arms sobbing. We've been spending most of our weekends together, which is wonderful, but when I ask him to do something on a weeknight, he always has an excuse. I swear, if it wasn't for the fact that I see him all weekend, I'd think he was married."

"That is a bit strange," admitted Suzy, "but honestly, Hope, I haven't seen you look this happy in a long time."

They lingered over lunch, catching up and gossiping about this and that.

As they were leaving they ran into Arlene, the fashion editor who was part of their Tomatoes group. "What are you ladies doing here?" she asked.

"Oh, we were just catching up. And you?"

"I was walking by and thought I'd pop in and see if they had a table for tonight. Luckily, they do, because we all know after Labor Day it will take weeks to get a reservation here."

"Well, lunch was wonderful. You'll enjoy dinner." And they all went their separate ways.

***

Suzy hadn't even arrived back at her office when she got an email from Arlene, who had actually introduced Suzy and Hope a few years back. Suzy and Hope had bonded instantly and been great friends since. And while she had always admired Arlene, she found her a bit aloof and difficult to really get to know. She was one of those people who carefully created her persona and you never knew who the real person was behind it.

She opened the email, which read, "Great seeing you and Hope today. I'd love to be included in your lunches sometime since I'm the one who brought you together."

Oh God, thought Suzy. *Are we still in high school?*

***

Trish had loved the Vermont getaway but now it was back to reality. And it wasn't a pretty one. She and Michael were sitting on their terrace reviewing all their expenses to see what they could cut and how they could stay afloat until they figured out how to get the cash flowing again.

She admitted she had no idea they had been spending at this level. Now that she was seeing things in black-and-white, she realized her monthly personal maintenance expenses alone were absurd.

There was her monthly salon visit to Frederic Fekkai with Frederic himself, five hundred dollars just for a haircut. There were her monthly appointments with New York City's top eyebrow shaping specialist, her twice-a-month facials, her personal trainer, her weekly mani and pedi, her yoga classes, her personal nutritionist, weekly massages, and her acupuncturist. And yes, she had to confess her occasional wrinkle-filler injections.

And then there was the shopping. If she saw a pair of shoes she liked, she'd buy it in every color. The personal shoppers at Saks and Bergdorf had her on speed dial to tell her when something that was just perfect for her had arrived in the store.

It averaged out to about five thousand dollars a month. She realized there were families living on that kind of income every month.

"All those expenses are going," she said to Michael. "I'm a do-it-yourself gal from now on. And no more shopping."

They agreed to drop their four club memberships at New York City's top private clubs, and their golf memberships at their elite clubs in Westchester and the Hamptons.

"And while you were gone, I got an offer on the Hamptons house," said Michael. "It's considerably below our asking price, and at the end of the season everyone is looking for a deal, but I think we should take it. It will give us enough to hopefully get us through the next few months, with lots of cuts to everything else. And we know it will take a while to sell the apartment. These damned co-ops have to approve everyone and they're very picky these days."

As much as it broke her heart to sell their beloved Hamptons house, Trish agreed. "Let's take the offer."

"I'm sorry I've been such a disappointment, Trish," said Michael dejectedly. "I'll get the sale going. I'm heading downtown."

One of Michael's friends from college had given him an office at his Wall Street firm so that Michael would have a base of operations to figure out what he was going to do next and at least still be in the thick of things.

"Will you be home for dinner?" asked Trish.

"No, I'm having dinner with a couple of guys from the Street."

"Michael, you're here less for dinner now than you were when you were working 24-7."

"Get off my case, Trish. I need to network." And with that he was out the door.

***

Madge's cell phone rang midafternoon on Wednesday. It was Jason. "I just got back into town. I'll pick you up at 6:00 p.m. Dress casually and wear flats."

"Where are we going?" asked Madge.

"It's a surprise."

"Okay, call me when you're in front of the building, and I'll pop right down."

By 6:00 p.m., Madge was in Jason's little red sports car and they were heading south on the West Side Highway. "So now can you tell me where we're going?"

"Sailing."

Ten minutes later they were at a dock at Chelsea Piers standing in front of a thirty-six-foot sailboat.

"Hop aboard," said Jason. And for the next two hours they sailed the Hudson, and then anchored for dinner.

Jason had brought a picnic basket with poached salmon, asparagus, a tossed salad, and Magnolia Bakery cupcakes.

"This is absolutely perfect," said Madge, as she sipped her wine and watched the sunset over the most beautiful city in the world.

"You're absolutely perfect," said Jason as he leaned in to kiss her.

Coming up for air he said, "Listen, I'm heading back to Vermont on Friday for Labor Day weekend. Come with me."

She thought about it for a minute. It wasn't as if she had to get to the studio, and nobody was answering emails or taking phone calls right now. *Oh, what the heck. Why not?* she decided to herself.

"I'd love that, Jason."

17

LABOR DAY WEEKEND SURPRISES

Suzy's actual fiftieth birthday was the Saturday of Labor Day weekend. Ken knew she wanted to lie low, but she did agree to his suggestion that they go to Gurney's Resort in Montauk for the weekend, for a quiet celebration with just the two of them. The kids had already headed back to college. He booked them a suite on the ocean.

They'd never cared much for the Hamptons scene, but they'd always loved Montauk. When their kids were growing up they spent two weeks there every summer. In those days it was still unspoiled, but now sadly, it was becoming Hamptons-ized too, with billionaires scooping up beachfront cottages and building their third or fourth mansions. Soon there would be no locals.

She knew she should be thankful she'd made it to fifty, and grateful for everything she had in her life — Ken, her wonderful kids, great friends. Which she was. But God, fifty seemed so old. She couldn't even say she was middle-aged because she'd have to live to be one hundred for that to be true. The AARP card in the mail had bummed her out — *How dare they do that?* And she actually found a long gray hair on her chin the other day in the ladies' room at the office. She plucked it before hopefully anyone had seen it.

She had a cute summer dress she was going to pack for the weekend that she hadn't worn since last summer. She decided to try it on first, and damn it, it didn't zip. She had loved her career and couldn't help wondering how the hell she had become the oldest person in the conference room. She was feeling invisible and marginalized too. She really needed this getaway with Ken.

They left early Friday morning and the second they hit Old Montauk Highway, Suzy started to feel more relaxed. Ken had arranged for an early check-in. The suite was beautiful and the first thing she did was open up the sliding glass doors to the terrace to smell the ocean breeze and watch the waves crest.

Ken came behind her, wrapped his arms around her waist and whispered in her ear, "You're the sexiest fifty-year-old I know."

God, she loved this man. The next thing she knew he was leading her to the king-size bed. They'd both been so busy she'd actually forgotten the last time they'd made love. Four weeks, six weeks?

Ken took his time exploring every inch of her body until her passion built. He entered her and their tempo increased. They climaxed almost simultaneously, something that rarely happened.

"Tell me again why we don't do this more often," said Ken.

"You're so right, sweetheart. I'm sorry I've been so distracted with work and everything else that's been going on with Trish and Madge. Thanks for getting us away this weekend."

They lay there in each other's arms listening to the waves crest, and made love again before lunch.

"Well, I guess we should actually leave the room," laughed Suzy, "and see this beautiful beach."

They spent the rest of the afternoon on lounge chairs under a beach umbrella on the beach. Suzy read the latest mystery best seller on her Kindle while Ken played in the surf like a kid. She didn't check her email once.

"I made a dinner reservation for seven tonight," said Ken when he returned from bodysurfing.

They headed back to the room, relaxed on the terrace with a bottle of wine and then took turns showering and dressing for dinner.

Ken took her hand as they headed out the door.

"Ken, the dining room is to the left," Suzy said as Ken started to lead her to the path to the beach.

"Not tonight. Follow me."

He led her down the beach a little bit and there was a cabana set up, with the front sides tied back revealing a beautifully set table with white linens, lanterns, and glistening stemware. And then to Suzy's utter surprise, she heard, "Happy birthday, Mom."

She turned around and there were her two beautiful children, Ian a freshman at Princeton, and Keri a junior at Boston College.

"You're supposed to be in school."

"We know, but then Dad thought it would be fun if we surprised you and now we all get to spend a weekend together in Montauk, just like when we were kids."

Tears ran down Suzy's cheeks. This was the best birthday surprise she could have imagined.

***

It was Saturday afternoon in the city. Trish had taken a subway (yes, the subway) to her gallery in the Village. You could tell it was a holiday weekend, because the normally bustling Village was relatively quiet. She was sitting at her desk in the gallery, looking at what was left of the latest exhibit by a very talented older black woman.

Tania was in her mideighties and had led a most interesting life. She had moved to New York from Montego Bay, Jamaica as a teenager. She got a scholarship to Barnard, and was a special ed teacher in the Bronx until she retired in her midfifties.

Her first loves had always been music and art. She took a few vocal lessons and discovered she had a natural knack for jazz. At sixty she started singing at open mics around the city, and then was invited to sing with a popular local jazz trio, which she continued to do, several nights a week.

At sixty-five she decided to take up painting. She took a few classes, and in no time, she was painting beautiful watercolors of her native Jamaica. Trish discovered her at an artists' sidewalk exhibit. They had sold nearly half of her paintings on opening night alone. Tania would always be eternally grateful to Trish for the opportunity. Every other gallery in town was only interested in young emerging artists.

Trish was deep in thought when Tania came through the gallery door.

"You're looking very pensive today," said Tania. "What's going on in that beautiful head of yours?"

Trish made them both some herbal tea, and then told Tania the brief version of her dire financial straits.

"The gallery rent is paid up for the next year," she told Tania, "but I need something else beyond the exhibits to make some money. I have an idea I want to run by you."

Trish had been thinking about this idea a lot lately, and Tania was the first to hear it.

"Tania, you're living proof that our lives don't stop at fifty, or when we 'retire', whatever the hell that means. So I was thinking, what if the gallery could become a place for inspiring women at any age to try new things, and to live healthy lives too. You would be a wonderful guest speaker. And I have my nutritionist, my personal trainer, and my acupuncturist who would all be terrific too."

"I love it," said Tania. "An inspiration and wellness center for women."

"Yes, exactly," said Trish excited by the idea.

***

Jason put the top down on the little red convertible and they headed up the thruway to Vermont. They stopped for lunch at an adorable little roadside restaurant that was on a lake, off the thruway.

"You know, Jason, I'm not much of a country girl but this is beautiful. And you should know I don't even know how to drive, so I don't know how I'd fare in your neck of the woods."

Jason was incredulous. "You don't drive?"

"Well, I grew up in New York City and I went to college at NYU. My family didn't even own a car," said Madge. "So yes, I never learned to drive."

"We're going to remedy that this weekend," laughed Jason.

An hour and a half later, they were driving up the long gravel drive to Jason's house.

"We're home," said Jason.

Madge actually liked the sound of that.

They headed inside. "Come on," said Jason, carrying her overnight bag upstairs. "Tonight, you don't have to come knocking on my door."

They put her things in his third-floor bedroom.

They went back down to the kitchen where Bertha greeted them. "I've got a chicken roasting in the oven, and some sides you just need to heat up. The salad's all made. You just have to dress it."

"Sounds perfect, Bertha. I need to check on a couple of things. Why don't you stay here, Madge, and keep Bertha company for a few minutes," and with that Jason headed out the door.

"Bertha, how long have you worked for Jason?"

"Well, I've known him since he was a kid. My dad used to help his grandpa out with the farm, and I used to babysit Jason and Chrissy. So, we go back a long ways."

"You must have been pleased then, when Jason bought the farm back."

"Oh, I was thrilled," said Bertha. "And when he and Abigail started renovating the place, Jason reached out to see if I'd help out with the cooking and cleaning." She stopped suddenly, realizing she'd said too much.

"Well, I need to get home. Everything's set for dinner. Nice seeing you again."

Abigail. That must be the professor, thought Madge. *And it must have been really serious if she helped him renovate this house.*

"Hey, sunshine," Jason said as he strolled back into the kitchen. "Where's Bertha?"

"She went home."

"Well, that chicken has a way to go. So, come outside Miss City Girl. I'm going to give you your first driving lesson."

They headed toward the barn where Jason had an old Jeep. He backed it out and then changed seats with Madge. She'd never been so nervous in her life. He gave her a few basic pointers, and she gently put her foot on the accelerator.

"Oh my God, I'm actually driving."

They tooled around the farm for about an hour, and then drove back to the barn.

"Well-done, City Girl. Tomorrow we'll try you out on a real road."

The rest of the weekend flew by. Saturday and Sunday were beautiful summerlike days. Jason drove her around the country roads of Vermont and showed her some of his favorite little towns and his favorite skiing places. They drove to Stratton Mountain, Okemo, and Killington. Madge had skied out West a few times, but never in New England.

"This winter, you'll have to try Vermont skiing. Although we do get icy trails sometimes, so it can be a little more daunting than skiing in the West," Jason had said to her.

At night there was a chill in the air and it felt more like fall. She and Jason sat around his fire pit, enjoyed a brandy after dinner, and talked about everything. Well almost everything, before heading upstairs. They were starting to know each other's bodies and what each of them liked, and their lovemaking kept getting better.

On Sunday night back at the fire pit after dinner, Jason said, "I can't believe we have to head back to the city tomorrow. This has been a wonderful weekend, Madge."

"It really has, Jason. I never thought I could love the country so much. Or learn to drive." They both laughed.

A silence hung over them for a few minutes, and Madge finally said, "Jason, listen. We have to talk about the elephant in the room. I know you had a love and lost her. And I know her imprint and

91

memories are in this house. Please, if I'm not intruding, tell me about her."

Jason sighed. "Yes, Madge, I was planning on telling you about Abigail. Even after three years, it's still so raw sometimes I can't catch my breath. But since I've met you, I feel like for the first time in three years that life can matter again."

Jason then told her the story. Abigail Gordon was a popular literature professor at Harvard. He was in her English lit class his sophomore year.

"I was always such a geek that I thought reading fiction was a waste of time. But Abigail had the most wonderful way of bringing the characters to life and relating their struggles to ours. That was the year I fell in love with literature and with Abigail too. She'd have these discussion groups at her apartment on campus and invite several of us for dinner and conversation.

"I learned her schedule, so I could 'accidently run into her' when she was having coffee, or sitting on a bench in the quad. And we'd talk. She was the first one I told about my idea for Snazzed. She thought it was brilliant. She became my mentor and friend, and at that time my love was definitely unrequited.

"She had a lovely home up in the woods not too far from here too. I'd meet her there when I came up skiing, and we'd hike through the woods and then she'd make me lunch or dinner. In my junior year when the VCs wanted to start throwing money at

Snazzed, I thought about leaving school. She was the one who encouraged me to get my degree first, one of the best things I ever did.

"It wasn't until four years after I graduated that we became romantically involved. I had loved her all along. I was twenty-five and she was forty-five. She worried about the age difference and that she had been my professor, but really none of that mattered. You see, Madge, I've never been interested in women my age, and certainly not younger women. I don't even know what to say to women in their twenties. They're just not interesting because they haven't lived enough of life yet, and their values are still developing. I guess you could say I'm an old soul.

"By then Snazzed was growing like crazy. Abigail kept me grounded, and her cottage was my escape from the insane tech world. When my grandparents' place came back on the market six years ago, I called the Realtor that day and paid over the asking amount. Abigail helped with the restoration. We'd spend weekends scouring the barn sales and antiques stores. A lot of what you see in the house are our finds.

"And then four years ago, we got the horrible news that she had cancer again. Several years ago, Abigail had breast cancer and she was way past the five-year survival marker. But this time, the cancer metastasized in her lungs. The prognosis was grim. I took her to every leading cancer specialist in the country, but they all said the same thing. I wanted to take her to Europe where they were doing a lot of experimental treatments, but she refused. And then she refused all treatments. She spent a year living her life while she died. But she lived every moment of it with joy and gratefulness. She died three years ago.

"Madge, you coming into my life is the first joy I've felt since then. I love having you in this house, and I know that Abigail would have wanted that too."

By this time, Jason's voice was quivering, and his eyes were glistening.

Madge just took his hand, and they quietly watched the embers fade.

It was a quiet ride back to the city the next day. Madge was glad that Jason had finally opened up his heart to her, but she couldn't help feeling that Abigail still owned a very large part of it.

Jason dropped her off at her place and they made plans to have dinner later in the week. Madge entered the apartment, dropped her things in the bedroom, poured herself a glass of wine, and then turned on her computer.

She couldn't help herself. She Googled "Abigail Gordon" and then clicked the first image. There, staring back at her, was her own reflection. Now she understood the uncomfortable looks she had gotten when she first met Chrissy and Bertha.

She and Abigail Gordon could be twins. *Oh my God, he's trying to bring Abigail back from the dead.*

18

THE SUMMIT

It had been a rough couple of weeks for Madge. After the shock of seeing Abigail Gordon's photo and not sleeping that night, she had texted Jason the next morning and suggested they meet in Central Park. She wanted to be on neutral ground when she told Jason she couldn't be his reincarnated dead lover. She had told him as gently as she could, but he was devastated.

"I admit the initial attraction was your resemblance to Abigail, but that's where the resemblance ends. It's you, Madge, that I've fallen in love with," Jason pleaded with her.

"Jason, you're a great guy. But you're still living in the past and I can't live with those ghosts." With that she walked away without looking back for fear she'd change her mind.

As if breaking up with Jason wasn't difficult enough, her phone hadn't exactly been ringing off the hook with offers, unless you count the local New York City station that wanted to hire her for the evening news roundup at about one third of what she had been making. Right now the only thing she had going was hosting the New York City Public Library's annual fall gala at the end of October, which she did gratis. Assuming they still wanted her.

Maybe this Reinvention & Rejuvenation Summit she had reluctantly agreed to go to with Trish and Madge and some of the other Tomatoes would help get her out of her funk.

The summit was the idea of Ginny Dalton, a fortysomething, sometime actress, now turned lifestyle guru. She was the daughter of a famous actress and a father who was a top director, which made her Hollywood royalty. She had teamed up with Catherine Mudge, the editor of *Reinvent*, a magazine whose mission was to convince women over forty that they had to continually reinvent themselves to prevent becoming irrelevant.

Madge personally felt that was a lot of bullshit and sent a message saying, 'who you are isn't good enough, so become something different'. But here she was on Saturday morning, standing in the lobby of the Grand Hyatt where the Tomatoes had agreed to meet. In addition to Madge and Trish, Hope (the Broadway producer) was joining them, as was Arlene (the fashion editor), Celeste (the romance novelist), and Marilyn (the restauranteur.) Quite the group of accomplished impressive women, none of whom needed to be reinvented. Yet here they were.

As soon as they had all assembled they headed up to the main ballroom.

Shortly after 9:00 a.m., Ginny and Catherine walked onto the stage to thunderous applause. Apparently, Ginny had quite the devotees. The Tomatoes had taken note of all the size zero blondes with long straight highlighted hair like Ginny's, all dressed in their cute little yoga outfits.

Ginny took the microphone and promised the audience a day that would lead them to the path of mental clarity, physical energy, improved focus and attitude. Catherine chimed in that it was their hope that attendees would leave with a renewed sense of motivation and purpose, feeling centered and spiritually aligned.

Celeste leaned over to Madge and whispered, "This sounds like a cult."

Ginny announced that the first panel, "Sexuality and Spirituality", would be moderated by Heather Stone.

Madge groaned hearing the name of her nemesis. Just when she thought this day couldn't get worse, "Ms. Big Tits in the Camera" was in the house.

The next panel was "Rejuvenation Trends at Spas". Madge, Suzy, and Trish almost fell out of their chairs when the moderator introduced Kimmy Hanes, Director of the acclaimed Green Mountain Spa in Vermont. Kimmy talked about the benefits of colonics and "digestive release" massages.

Madge could hear Suzy stifling a giggle and didn't dare look her way.

The panel discussions and featured speakers continued throughout the morning. The last panel before lunch was called "Love Your Vagina". Ginny moderated this one and the panelists included an energy healer and a doctor who specializes in cosmic flow of the vagina. When they got into a discussion on the benefits of vaginal steaming and how inserting jade eggs into your vagina can cultivate sexual energy, Hope passed a note to Celeste who passed it on to the rest of them, that read, "Let's get the hell out of here." One by one, they made their way quietly out of the ballroom into the lobby. As soon as they were all there, Hope said, "Jade eggs and vaginal steaming?" and they all broke into hysterical laughter.

"Oh my God," said Celeste still laughing, "I need to get to the ladies' room before I pee in my pants."

They all made a quick retreat for bladder relief and makeup repairs. When Hope suggested they ditch the rest of the summit and head to Sardi's for lunch they were all in.

Just as Madge was leaving the ladies' room, in walked Heather Stone. "Madge, what a surprise to see you here. Looking for a little inspiration for your next act? We all miss you so much. I hope you are doing well," she purred in her most solicitous voice.

"Thanks for your concern, Heather. You'll be the first to know my next move," said Madge as she exited the ladies' room.

***

They were still laughing about the absurdity of the program when their lunches arrived. "And to think we paid five hundred dollars to hear this crap," said Arlene.

"And those were for the peon seats," added Marilyn. "The Ginny look-alikes paid a thousand dollars so they can have herbal tea with her this afternoon."

"Well, I wasn't going to say anything yet," said Trish, "but after sitting through so much nonsense this morning, I want to run a new business idea for my gallery by you all."

They listened intently as Trish shared the idea for a Women's Inspiration and Wellness Center. "I'd start out once or twice a month with one or two experts on different topics. But these experts would be the real deal. Leading experts in health, nutrition, and wellness. And stories of women like Tania who inspire all of us to never let our dreams die, and that we can achieve so much at any age."

"I love it," Celeste said first.

"Me too," said Suzy, "and this is perfect for you, Trish. You've always been ahead of the curve on healthy living and you're so knowledgeable."

"And maybe we could film some of these inspiring women who can change the perception of how we think of older women, and create a YouTube channel," added Madge. "I can help with that."

"Well, I'll certainly help get people there," said Hope.

"And I could do some PR for you," added Arlene. "I have a lot of contacts in the wellness field too."

By the time checks came, everyone was excited about Trish's idea and looking for ways they could contribute.

As the others were leaving, Trish asked Suzy and Madge if they could stay a little longer. "Let's grab a Starbucks," she suggested. "The chai lattes are on me."

Settled at a small table, Trish said, "Listen, sorry to spring that on you at lunch. You were the first two I wanted to talk to about my idea, but I got so excited I couldn't help myself. And I really could use your help and more importantly I'd like you to be part of this."

"Actually," said Suzy, "I think it was great that you shared it with the group today. You know that Madge and I will always support whatever you want to do, but their genuine excitement was a wonderful endorsement of your idea.

"Here's a thought. You know I lead brainstorming sessions at the agency all the time. Why don't you both come to Bronxville tomorrow," suggested Suzy. "I'll serve Sunday brunch and then let's do a brainstorming session and see where it leads us."

19

THE THREE TOMATOES IS HATCHED

After brunch, Suzy led Trish and Madge into the family room where she had set up a large easel and pad. She gave each of them sticky notes, and a package of red and green dots.

"So, we want to take this idea of inspiring women to live their dreams at any age, and to live healthy fulfilling lives, and brainstorm what that means and what that could look like. I'm going to write all our ideas on the easel, no matter how wacky or out there they sound," explained Suzy. "Then we'll review them, and each of us will put red dots on the ones to ditch, and green dots on the ideas with potential. Then we can start to build a plan."

When Ken got home from his golf game later that afternoon, he was impressed to see the walls of the family room covered with sheets of easel paper. "Well, looks like you three have had quite a productive afternoon," he said walking in and giving each of them a hug and kiss.

"Oh, Ken, you have no idea," said Trish. "Madge and Suzy have the most brilliant ideas."

"Well, you were the seed, Trish," said Madge.

"Don't let me interrupt," said Ken. "And if you want me to order pizza for you later, or make drinks, I'm happy to be cabana boy," he laughed.

By nine o'clock that night they had outlined a business plan. They would form a corporation called The Three Tomatoes a lifestyle media brand for smart, savvy grownup women. They'd have a website with content from experts in fields that included fashion, style, health, travel, dating, life, and finding your next endeavor. They'd create newsletters to drive traffic to the website and to promote the events they would launch at Trish's gallery. Madge and Suzy knew how important video would be since that was the new content model that was driving the Internet. Madge was already talking about getting video of the first events, doing video interviews, and creating their own YouTube channel.

They spent quite a while discussing the model for how to make this a profitable business. Madge and Suzy agreed that the best source of revenues would be from advertising and sponsorships.

"That's why it will be important to build an audience not just with numbers, but with demographics that will appeal to marketers," said Madge. "In fact, I did an on-air segment not long ago that said women over fifty are the healthiest, wealthiest, most educated, and active generation of women ever. And over the next decade, we'll control two-thirds of consumer wealth from our own assets and from parents and spouses."

"Then why the heck are we still invisible to most marketers?" asked Trish.

"That's the million-dollar question, Trish," said Suzy, "which is why I think another piece of this business could be consulting to marketers who want to reach, or should be reaching, this important segment of women.

"Also, the tone we set is very important. We're not preaching and not empowering anyone, and let's strike the word *reinvention* from our vocabularies. God knows, these women are successful and accomplished and already have power. No one needs to be reinvented. We want this to be a conversation with friends who are going through similar issues as we age. We're in this together and we're there to be their cheerleaders."

"Yes," agreed Trish. "And we want them to trust that we're providing them with expert advice that's realistic and practical, not the latest fads and trends from celebrities or advice from twentysomething bloggers."

"And let's ban the word *networking* too," added Madge. "I think we've all had enough of events where everyone is running around handing out business cards and trying to give their elevator pitch over cocktails. We want our events to be social, and for people to meet organically."

"Our events should feel like our Ripe Tomato dinners. Like you've been invited to an evening out with friends to meet some of their friends, have fun and interesting conversations," Trish added.

Over the objections of Trish and Suzy, Madge insisted on seeding the start-up with fifty thousand dollars. "Listen, I've been paid a lot of money over the years. I don't have a husband or kids, and I've been too much of a workaholic to even take vacations, so I have a shit-load of money sitting in investments and I can't think of anything I'd rather invest in more than a venture with the three of us."

They agreed on next steps. Suzy had a great female creative director in the agency she could hire freelance to design the logo and start working on a website. They had decided to do a "soft launch" with a first event in early January at Trish's gallery. Madge already had a video guy in mind to film it too.

"I can create the first newsletter that promotes the event," said Suzy, "And we'll get all our friends to help promote the event and that will be the start of our database.

"This calls for a champagne toast." Suzy opened a bottle of Perrier-Jouët, and they all clinked glasses.

"To new beginnings," said Madge. "And who knows, maybe we'll even change the perception of aging in our hyper youth-oriented culture."

20

THE LIBRARY BECOMES MORE PUBLIC

The past month had been a beehive of activity for the Tomatoes trio. Suzy had been working evenings with Amy, one of the agency's brilliant creative directors, whom she hired freelance to work with her surreptitiously on the logo design and initial website for The Three Tomatoes.

Amy had loved the concept and got it immediately. "You know, Suzy, I really admire your generation of women. You led the way for my generation to have a lot fewer doors closed on us," Amy had said. "Plus, you still look great, and you're cool without trying to be. I want to be a Tomato when I grow up." And both she and Suzy had laughed.

Amy had created a modern sleek logo just using the words *The Three Tomatoes* and avoiding the obvious image of an actual tomato. "You'd look like a gardening site," she had said. And she added Suzy's tagline, "The insiders' guide for women who aren't kids."

She created a template for a website that could be expanded over time, but initially could be used to promote upcoming events, take payments, and invite people to sign up for the newsletters.

Even with the extra hours of work on top of her day job, Suzy felt an exhilaration she hadn't felt in a long time. Ken had even remarked that she seemed more energized these days.

And she loved her weekly update meetings with Trish and Madge.

They were all excited about the first event. It was titled, "That's *Not* All, Folks", a jab at Madge's former magazine show, *That's All, Folks*. Madge would moderate, but she'd start off by talking about her personal experience of "jumping off the cliff", not knowing how she'd land, and the uncertainties she still felt. Then she'd interview Tania.

They'd start the event with an hour of socializing with wine and hors d'oeuvres and then have the program — about forty-five minutes to allow for questions, and then more socializing. Madge had called a couple of her film crew friends, who all adored and missed her, and they were excited to film the event. She actually had to insist they be paid.

The event was set for early January and there were still a lot of details to finalize.

***

Madge had been so busy planning The Three Tomatoes event, she'd barely had time to think about her hosting duties for the library benefit tonight. She had finally gotten around to reviewing the notes, and who she'd be introducing. When she showed up for the event walk-through earlier in the day, the library president hemmed and hawed a bit and then finally said, "Madge, how shall I introduce you?"

The event promotion had already gone out describing Madge as the Emmy-winning host of the *Good Morning New York* show and cohost of *That's All, Folks*.

"Well, I guess you say, here's Madge, the over-the-hill broadcaster looking for her next gig," she laughed. He looked aghast. "Why don't you just say, 'journalist Madge Thompson', that should do it."

A month ago, she wouldn't have been able to joke about the "over-the-hill broadcaster" thing. At that point, she was feeling like quitting had been the worst mistake she'd ever made. But then she started to think about how wrapped up her identify was in what she did, not who she was. But who was she really? She was still working on that one, but The Three Tomatoes had given her a new sense of purpose.

And then, there were continual thoughts of Jason. One of the things she most admired about him was that despite his enormous business success, he didn't define himself by what he did. Snazzed was a business, not his life, which he seemed to be getting on with quite well these days. A Page Six item reported he had been seen out and about with a rotating bevy of beauties. "I guess he got over me quickly," she had said flippantly to Suzy and Trish, as if it meant nothing to her. They knew differently.

She looked at herself in the mirror. She loved the beautiful red satin slip dress that her designer friend Gab had made for her. It showed off her buff arms and hinted sensuously at all of her curves. Her beautiful brunette hair was cascading in curls around her face. *Not too bad for an old broad,* she thought.

Hmmm...Gab would be a great person to interview too for The Three Tomatoes. She had the most wonderful approach to dressing women of all ages and shapes and everyone who walked into her boutique in Midtown left feeling beautiful even if they didn't buy a thing. That was Gab's special talent.

She had also dressed Marilyn for tonight. Marilyn knew she'd run into her cheating, lying ex-husband with his now live-in girlfriend, who was the former hostess of her family's iconic restaurant, and was twenty years younger than Marilyn. Madge convinced Marilyn to go the event and to treat herself to a Gab creation. Gab's motto for divorced women running into hubbies who were dating women younger than their daughters was, "Clothes are the best revenge."

Madge grabbed her bag and headed to the elevator.

***

Trish had been so busy she had hardly seen Michael in the past few days. They were like ships passing in the night. And when she tried to tell him about The Three Tomatoes, his eyes glazed over and he muttered comments like, "Interesting concept."

She was dressing from her closet tonight. This was the first library benefit that she hadn't purchased something new to wear. When she perused her walk-in closet and the section that had her formal wear, she was appalled at herself. *How could I have shopped so mindlessly like this?* There were at least thirty couture dresses she had worn exactly one time, and enough Manolos, Jimmy Choos, and Louboutins to start her own shoe store. She decided on a royal blue satin princess-cut dress, very Audrey Hepburn, that complemented her petite frame and red hair, which she had in an upsweep.

Michael walked into her dressing room, looking very handsome in his custom-made tux. "Trish, you take my breath away."

Thank God, he had finally noticed she was alive.

***

"Well, you are one hot tomato," Ken said, as he appreciatively looked at Suzy from head to toe. She was dressed in a short black cocktail dress and four-inch Louboutins that showed off her great legs. The last thing to go, she thought. Her long straight blond hair caressed her shoulders.

"Well, you're not so bad yourself," she said to Ken who hadn't gained an ounce since his college days, and still had all his hair. "I guess we're still Ken and Barbie," a moniker their friends jokingly used to describe them.

"Yes, we are the dashing couple. May I escort you to the prom?"

And out they walked to the waiting limo.

***

The grandiose steps of the Fifth Avenue library were glittering with tea light candles as the guests made their way up the stairs of this beaux arts architectural masterpiece, one of the most impressive buildings in New York City, and the country for that matter. They entered the library foyer with its marble floors and towering ceilings, where cocktails and passed hors d'oeuvres were being served to New York City's social and business elite.

Ken's firm had bought a VIP table for twenty-five thousand dollars and he had invited Trish and Michael to join them, along with some of his clients. At moments like this, Suzy couldn't help thinking how far she'd come from the Levittown house she grew up in. Her Brooklyn-born parents had bought it so they could raise their children in the country. Now of course, the irony was that her parents' modest Brooklyn neighborhood had restored brownstones selling in the millions, and Levittown was just another overcrowded, middle-class suburb surrounded by strip malls.

Several of the Ripe Tomatoes had chipped in for the ten-thousand-dollar table. Hope and her boyfriend, Marvin, Celeste, Arlene and her husband, and Marilyn would be seated together, along with a few other friends.

They had agreed to find each other during cocktails.

Suzy spotted Hope and a very good-looking man whom she assumed was Marvin. She made her way over.

"Hope, you look fabulous," Suzy said. And she did. Hope had a great flare for style and drama and was dressed in a stunning gold lamé wrap gown that accented her ample cleavage. She was wearing oversize dangling earrings and her megawatt smile was amplified by her bright red lipstick.

"And so do you, darling. Let me introduce Marvin."

"It's a pleasure to meet you, Suzy. Hope sings your praises all the time," said the very charming Marvin.

They were soon joined by Trish, Celeste, Arlene, and Marilyn.

"Marilyn, you look smoking hot," said Hope, and they all agreed.

Gab had dressed Marilyn in the most beautiful head-to-toe teal chiffon creation that gave the illusion of an angel floating on a cloud, which contrasted perfectly with her Christian Louboutin fuck-me pumps. She exuded a self-confidence they hadn't seen from her since her messy divorce.

Celeste looked around the room in her keen observational way that made her such a great writer, and said, "Look at these air-kissing phonies. They don't even look each other in the eye when they're making small talk because they're too busy scanning the room for someone more important to talk to than you."

"And speaking of the phonies, here comes the biggest of them all," Hope chimed in as Ellen Martin, whom Hope was sure was the evil note-writer, approached the group.

Air-kisses were exchanged, and then Ellen zeroed in on Marvin. "And who is this charming man?"

Hope put her arm territorially in Marvin's, and introduced him to Ellen.

"You look very familiar, have we met?" Ellen inquired in her whiny nasally voice.

Before Marvin could answer, Hope said, "Oh look. There's Catherine Dubois. I haven't seen her in ages." Off she went with Marvin, leaving Ellen looking slightly puzzled.

"Hope, how wonderful to see you. You always look so vivacious," said the always gracious Catherine.

"I'm very well. And this is my friend, Marvin."

They chatted a bit, and then Hope couldn't help but say, "Catherine, I'm so sorry you missed our workshop in July for a wonderful show I hope to get to Broadway one of these days."

Catherine looked confused. "I don't understand. I was all set to attend when I ran into Ellen Martin the day before, and she told me you had pulled the plug on the show."

Hope hid her furor. "Well, clearly there was a misunderstanding. I only *just* postponed the financing for that show to focus on another very exciting show I'm working on. I'd love to tell you about it."

"I'd love to hear more," said Catherine. "Call me next week."

"That bitch Ellen," Hope said to Marvin as Catherine walked away. "I knew she sabotaged me."

"It will all work out, my dear," said Marvin in his usual calm way.

The bells started to chime indicating that the guests should make their way upstairs to their assigned tables.

Suzy, Ken, Trish, and Michael made their way to their VIP table that was near the front of the stage. They had just sat down, when Trish leaned over to Suzy and said, "Look who's at the next table."

It was Jason, in all his handsome glory, who had also bought a VIP table. He spotted Trish and Suzy and headed their way.

They introduced him to their husbands, and they all made polite small talk before Jason returned to his table.

The lights flickered to indicate the program would start, and then the president of the library board walked out onstage to greet the boisterous, alcohol-fueled crowd who were still chatting and mingling at other tables.

It took him a few minutes to quiet the crowd down, say a few words, and then announce the emcee for the evening, "Emmy award-winning journalist, Madge Thompson."

Madge walked onto the stage in her fabulous red dress to enthusiastic applause.

She took the mic and opened with, "Now if only that applause had translated to ratings I wouldn't be looking for a job right now." The audience laughed out loud, and she had put everyone at ease.

She then went on to talk about how important the library was to New York City, and all the good work they do. "Enjoy your dinner and I'll be back shortly to introduce you to this evening's honorees."

Suzy had watched Jason who never took his eyes off Madge. It almost seemed like he was in a trance. She leaned over and whispered to Trish, "He's got it bad."

Madge had immediately spotted Jason too and her heart had skipped a beat. *Calm down, girl,* she told herself. She knew it was inevitable that they'd run into each other somewhere. She just hoped he'd leave after the awards and not stay for the after-dinner drinks and desserts back in the lobby.

She deliberately stayed backstage during dinner and then returned to the stage to introduce the honorees.

"Well, that was another wonderful event," Ken said as they all made their way back to the lobby. They all agreed.

Their Ripe Tomatoes group had reconvened with brandies and Baileys Irish Cream, when Madge appeared and made her way slowly to them as well-wishers stopped to chat with her.

"You were fabulous," said Ken as Madge finally got to their group. But within seconds Madge was surrounded by more well-wishers and Trish and Suzy couldn't even get to her.

Madge was starting to feel smothered when she saw a chance to make a break for the ladies' room. She had just taken a couple of steps into the long hallway leading to the restrooms, when she felt a light touch on her elbow. She turned to face Jason.

"Madge, you look beautiful and you charmed the entire room tonight."

"Thanks, Jason, that's kind of you to say."

"It's not just kindness, Madge," he said wistfully. "Listen, I know I screwed things up, but at least have breakfast with me. I miss talking to you."

She sighed. "All right. But just breakfast," and then she continued her walk to the ladies' room. *Here I go again,* she thought.

By the time she got back to the foyer she was able to make her way to Trish and Suzy and a large group that included the Ripe Tomatoes, Celeste DuBois, and a few society-type Bergdorf Blondes, with pulled faces and bony bodies. She quickly scoured the room and didn't see any signs of Jason.

Hope was holding court and telling a very funny story about a well-known actor who had three testicles. Just as she was getting to the punch line, Ellen Martin suddenly appeared and loudly said to Marvin, "Oh now I know where we've met. It's been bugging me all night." Everyone got silent. "You're the bartender during the week at the New York Athletic Club. You always remember exactly what my husband and I drink." And with that she flew away on her broom.

Hope had turned white. Suzy immediately grabbed her arm and Madge quickly whispered, "Follow me. There's a small private room in back of the stage."

Madge handed Hope the brandy she had carried with her.

"I have never been so humiliated in my life. How could she? And how could he lie to me? No wonder he couldn't meet me on weeknights. I had no idea. Now she'll tell everyone, and I'll be a laughingstock," said Hope fighting back tears. "I can't go back out there."

"Don't worry," said Suzy, "We'll stay here until the crowd has left."

Madge sent a quick text to Trish to give them the all clear when the foyer emptied.

"I'll get even with her," Hope vowed, "if it's the last thing I do." And this time Suzy and Madge knew this wasn't just Hope, the drama queen, and they agreed with her.

21

MIXED THANKS

It was the week before Thanksgiving, and the Ripe Tomatoes were at their usual haunt for their monthly dinner. They had all been relieved to get Hope's email reminder, since she had been under the radar after the library shit storm. Suzy had reached out to her, but Hope said she just needed some alone time and the only person she was seeing was her shrink. "I love you dearly, Suzy. You're a real friend, but I just need to get through this on my own."

Hope made her grand entrance, late as usual, but she looked ebullient, which was a surprise and a relief to all of them.

With dinner ordered, Hope said, "I have exciting news."

She then told them about bringing Celeste's story to Broadway. "It's called *If Tomorrow Never Comes*. Celeste and a wonderful up and coming playwright finished the play in record time, and we already have a couple of beautiful original songs, and the rest of the score is almost done. And we have a fabulous director who is just about to come on board, but I can't say who yet."

Celeste chimed in, "I never thought at this point in my life I'd be working on a Broadway play, and I have to thank Hope for her vision on this one. It's the most exciting thing I've ever done."

"But wait, there's more," continued Hope. "I gave the play to Catherine Dubois and she fell in love with it. She's coming in as our lead investor. And she's putting together a group of her überwealthy friends in Palm Beach over Thanksgiving weekend, and she's invited Celeste and me to pitch the show. We're bringing a couple of performers and the songwriters too and we'll do a little preview for them. Catherine thinks we'll have the money raised to start our workshops in January and get this baby to an off-Broadway theater for an opening this spring. Now we just need a couple of 'names' for the lead roles."

The group was so excited, they all started talking at once.

"Tomatoes, I propose a toast," said Madge, "To the awesome duo of Hope and Celeste and to a Tony Award in your future. And by the way, can I invest in the show too?"

"Well, I think we'd be happy to start off with an Obie Award and then on to Broadway and a Tony. But we could let you in on the action, Madge, and anyone else who's interested," laughed Hope.

They clinked glasses all around the table.

"Trish and Madge and I have an announcement to make too," said Suzy. Everyone got quiet again. "Remember Trish's idea of an inspiration and wellness center for women? Well we're turned the idea into a media venture. It's called The Three Tomatoes, and it's a lifestyle brand that caters to women like us."

Suzy, Trish, and Madge shared the initial concept, and the group loved it.

"We're launching with our first event in early January and we hope you'll all help spread the word to your friends," said Trish.

After promises of support around the table, Celeste raised her glass and said, "Here's to the Ripe Tomatoes. You are a wonderful supportive group and I value your friendships. I am grateful to each one of you. Happy Thanksgiving!"

They all exchanged hugs, kisses, and Happy Thanksgiving wishes and headed on their way.

It was a crisp fall night and Madge decided to walk back to her Murray Hill apartment. She needed the long walk to clear her head. The Three Tomatoes launch plans were moving along well. They had set up an office in Trish's gallery and it was great to have a place to go to every morning again. Suzy joined them there for status meetings once a week, usually in the evening. They already had ideas for a second event, and were starting to reach out to various experts to invite them to be contributors to the website. They couldn't pay anyone at this point, but surprisingly almost everyone was enthusiastic and saw contributing as another way to promote their own brands.

But tonight, as she walked home, it was Jason she had on her mind. They'd had breakfast a couple of times since the library event. Jason had played it very low-key, and hadn't suggested anything beyond breakfast. She shared The Three Tomatoes idea with him. He had listened intently, asked a lot of really smart questions, particularly on the business model side, and shared some great advice too. He even offered to invest in the new company, but Madge said she thought for right now they were okay with the seed money she'd put into their venture.

She was almost home when her cell phone rang. It was Jason.

"Hey. Did I catch you at a bad time?"

"Nope, I was just walking home from dinner."

"Well, I just wanted to wish you a Happy Thanksgiving. I'm heading to Vermont tomorrow and I'll stay there through Thanksgiving. Maybe we can have breakfast when I get back?"

"Happy Thanksgiving to you and Chrissy too. And breakfast sounds good."

There was a pause, and then Jason said, "You know we'd love to have you there for Thanksgiving."

"Thanks, Jason, but I always spend Thanksgiving with Suzy and her family. Have a good week."

As soon as Jason hung up, she thought about how wonderful Thanksgiving in Vermont with Jason would be. But the thought of being there with the ghost of Abigail brought her back to reality.

***

Suzy loved Thanksgiving. It was her favorite holiday. Unlike the stress of Christmas, with presents and parties, and trying to jam good cheer into one month, Thanksgiving was about food, and family, and friends – and four days off from the agency.

Every morning she dreaded heading into the office. Especially right now since they were launching the new Arpello ads this weekend in time for the holidays, which was the make-or-break season for fragrances. Ryan was feeling the pressure. "The agency really needs this campaign to be a success," he had told Suzy, which was no surprise to her. They had lost a couple of major accounts since September, and Suzy had seen the grim P&Ls. She knew they'd be chopping heads before the holidays and it made her sick to her stomach. Thank goodness, she had her other job as chief strategist for The Three Tomatoes. It kept her going.

But this weekend she wasn't going to think about any of that. Her kids were home from college and her two best friends would be here shortly for Thanksgiving dinner, which she and Ken had hosted since the first year they got married. Trish and Madge had never missed one of them.

She walked into the kitchen where Ken was preparing the turkey for the oven. He loved this day too, and since the first year when she had put the turkey into the oven with the little plastic giblets package still inside, and the oven caught on fire, and they had to order Chinese takeout, Ken had taken over Thanksgiving dinner. They still laughed about it every year.

Suzy sat on one of the stools at the big center island counter, in their beautiful kitchen equipped with the best appliances and every cooking gadget known to mankind, and poured herself a glass of white wine. "You know, I still miss our first apartment."

Ken laughed, "Yes, I remember hauling groceries up the six flights. And two people couldn't be in the little closet-sized kitchen at the same time."

"I know. Little did we know that someday we'd be sitting in this spacious kitchen in a house with five bedrooms, a pool, and tennis courts having raised two great kids who are almost out of the house. I'm really grateful for all we have and the life we've built, but I miss those two romantic idealists we were back then."

"Yes, the years have flown by. That's why we need to enjoy every day. Real life intruded on the idealistic part, but we still have the romance," Ken said as he kissed the top of her head on his way to the oven with the stuffed bird.

Just then the doorbell rang. "That's got to be Madge or Trish," Suzy said. She heard Keri answer the door, and exclaim, "Aunt

Madge." Keri adored Madge, not to mention all the perks that came with being an adored "niece", like Madge getting her backstage at Justin Bieber and Katy Perry concerts.

Suzy made her way to the foyer and gave Madge a big hug too. "Come, let's sit in the living room by the fireplace. Keri, get your Aunt Madge a glass of wine."

Ian bounded downstairs to give Madge a huge bear hug. He was six-two and lifted Madge off her feet. "Now I feel old. I remember when I could lift you off your feet." They talked for a while about college and football. And then Ian left to call his high school girlfriend who was home from college too, to see if she wanted to hang out later. Even though they had agreed to see other people in college, they still cared about each other.

"Ah, young love," Suzy said, as Ian headed back upstairs. "Speaking of young love, Trish tells me you've been seeing Jason."

"You don't need to remind me that he's young. And we're not seeing each other in that sense. We've just had breakfast a couple of times. He's actually had some good business advice for The Three Tomatoes."

"Madge, you know I'm teasing you about the 'young' thing. The only person who has a problem with the age difference is you."

"If only it were just the age thing," said Madge. "That I could get over. He called me a few days ago and actually invited me to the farm for Thanksgiving. I told him I always spend Thanksgiving with you and Trish."

"Oh, Madge, you should have gone. We'd understand."

"I know you would. It's not that. The thought of meeting his family who all knew Abigail, and feeling like I'd be compared, isn't something I want to put myself through. It's just not meant to be."

Ken joined them. "Well, dinner will be ready in a couple of hours. I thought Trish and Michael would be here by now."

"Maybe they ran into traffic. I'll give Trish a call and see where they are."

Trish's cell phone rang several times and then went to voice mail. "That's strange," Suzy said.

A half an hour later Trish called back. "Suzy, it's me. I'm sorry I didn't answer before. But...but...I'm not going to make it for dinner."

"Trish, what are you talking about? What's going on?"

Trish started crying. "I found out last night that Michael's having an affair. I'm a mess and I'd be terrible company."

"Trish Hogan, you get in a car right now, or we're coming to get you."

Ken and Madge looked at Suzy.

"Trish found out that Michael's cheating on her."

***

Ken delayed dinner so that Suzy and Madge could talk to Trish. She wasn't exaggerating when she said she was a mess. Her hair was barely combed, she had mascara stains on her cheeks, and was dressed in yoga clothes.

"Okay, sweetie, start from the beginning," Suzy said after she made a cup of herbal tea for Trish.

"Well, you know, we hardly see each other. I've been so busy at the gallery and Michael gets home late just about every night, claiming he was with different Wall Street colleagues who have opportunities for him. And I admit I'm still angry that he never sat down and told me what was going on, so things have been strained. But last night he was in the shower, and his phone kept buzzing. He left it on the nightstand. So, I got up thinking it must be important, and there was a text message that said, 'I miss you already. You were wonderful tonight and I'll be thinking about you all day tomorrow.' And it was sent with a photo of her boobs.

"At first, I thought it was a hoax, but then I started scrolling through his texts," Trish said as she started crying again. "And there must have been twenty texts back and forth between them that are just too disgusting to repeat.

"He came back into the bedroom and saw me standing with his phone in my hand, and accusingly asked me what I was doing going through his phone. As if I were the guilty party! I just looked at him and told him he was a disgusting cheating bastard and to get out of the apartment. He tried to tell me it wasn't anything...just a stupid fling. I hurled a lot of awful words at him and a few physical items too, like his phone. He finally took his pillow and went into the guest room, because he said he has no place else to go.

"I couldn't sleep at all last night. And at 6:00 a.m. I went into the kitchen to get some coffee. He was just sitting there. I asked him to tell me who she is, and when this started, but he just sat there in silence and then walked out of the room, got dressed, and stormed out of the apartment."

Suzy and Trish sat there stunned.

"I don't know what I'm going to do. The co-op is sold, and Michael and I are supposed to move to our new place right after Christmas. Even with the sale of everything, we don't have enough money for two places. And I can't face seeing him, never mind living in the same space as him."

"You don't have to," said Madge, putting a reassuring arm around her friend. "I have a perfectly lovely guest room you can stay in as long as you like. We'll pick up a few of your things on the way home and you can move in tonight. It will be like old times."

"Oh, Madge, I don't even know what to say to you. You're a lifesaver."

"You'd do the same thing for me."

"Okay, Trish, let's get you up to my room and cleaned up a bit before dinner, so the kids aren't wondering what happened to Aunt Trish."

Trish somehow made it through dinner and put on her best face for Keri and Ian. She told them Uncle Michael wasn't feeling well. But she was really relieved to get in the Uber with Madge. The strain of pretending all was fine was just too much.

Madge told the driver they'd make a stop on Central Park West and asked him to wait a few minutes and then take them to Murray Hill. Madge went up with Trish. Fortunately, Michael hadn't returned, which was a good thing, because Madge would have given him a good piece of her mind. Trish threw a few things into a suitcase and then they headed downtown. It had been quite a Thanksgiving.

22

RECRIMINATIONS

When Trish didn't return home Thanksgiving night, Michael sent her several texts that she ignored. When he threatened to report her as missing, she finally texted back on Friday morning telling him she was staying with Madge.

Trish knew she couldn't avoid Michael forever. Sotheby's was showing up on Monday to appraise the artwork and antiques in the apartment. And they still had to pack and arrange for storage for items they were keeping but wouldn't fit in the one-bedroom apartment they rented on the Upper East Side.

She returned to the apartment Saturday morning to meet Michael and discuss their future, or at least the immediate one.

Michael looked like hell with dark circles under his eyes. Not that Trish looked much better.

Trish was seething on the inside, but as calmly as she could, told Michael her plan.

"I'll be here on Monday for the Sotheby walk-through and I'll make arrangements for what will go into storage. I'll schedule the moving company to move you into the new apartment the day after Christmas. I'll make arrangements for my clothes and personal belongings to be sent to the gallery. I have that back room where I can store them. And I'll be staying with Madge until I figure out what happens next." She was proud of herself for spewing that out without a single tear.

"Trish, this is crazy. You can't leave me after all these years. I love you. You're my best friend and I need you," Michael said pleadingly.

"This isn't how you treat your best friend, Michael. How could you do this? Explain that to me. With everything else that's happened and the fact that you held back the truth of our financial situation, now you cheat on me?" said Trish losing her cool. "And I'm supposed to forgive that? You're a lying, cheating son of a bitch and I hate your guts."

"Oh, and you're little Miss Perfect," Michael hurled back. "While I was busting my ass in the lion's den that's Wall Street, you were indulging yourself with couture clothes, massages, and your little art gallery. And you certainly didn't want to know a thing about my business or how we were paying for all this grandeur," said Michael, his voice getting louder and his face redder.

"And now for the past four months, all I feel is your pity. You look at me like I'm a total loser, which I guess I am. How do you think it makes me feel to be moving into a one-bedroom rental that's not even as nice as the one I owned when I first met you? And forget about intimacy. Is it any wonder that I succumbed to someone who looks at me like I'm still someone?"

"Oh, so now this is all my fault. That's just priceless, Michael. I'm getting a few of my things. Do not call or text me. I don't want to see your face until I have to on Monday morning."

"Fine," shouted Michael, as he stomped to the door.

"And I suppose you're headed to see your little chippie. Maybe you could move in with her, but she probably still has roommates."

With that, Michael stormed out and slammed the door.

***

Back at Madge's apartment later that day, Trish confessed that despite everything, she still loved Michael and wasn't at all sure she could just walk away.

"And you know, he did have a point or two. I have been harboring all this animosity toward him."

"Trish, don't you dare! His screwing around is not your fault."

"I know, I know. But his ego is at an all-time low. But I just don't think I have the emotional strength to put Humpty Dumpty back together again. "

"Listen," said Madge more gently this time. "Maybe you just need some time and space, and you've got that here. And we have a new venture to focus on."

"Yes, thank goodness for that. That's about all that's keeping me going right now. So let's talk about the event, and the types of interviews you want to do."

Madge started talking about a video series they could put on their YouTube channel called "Women of Substance". They were both excited about this idea and before they knew it the afternoon had flown by, and they had a great list of potential interviewees.

Madge poured them each a glass of wine. "Hey, you know what we need to do?"

"Oh no, I see that look in your eyes," laughed Trish, for the first time today.

"We need to get all dressed up and head somewhere fun. My treat, and I know just the spot."

Two hours later they were at one of the hottest restaurants and jazz clubs in Harlem. They ordered martinis at the bar, and before they even finished their first drinks, they had three guys wanting to buy them another round.

It was three o'clock in the morning when they stumbled back into Madge's apartment, tipsy and still laughing.

"Oh, Madge, that was exactly what I needed. I haven't been hit on in so long I didn't even know I was being hit on."

"Well, it was good to see you still remember how to flirt, Trish. And if I hadn't seen you dancing on the table, I wouldn't have believed it."

"I'm sure I'll regret this in the morning, but right now I feel alive for the first time in quite a while."

The next morning Madge was the one with regrets. There on Page Six was a photo of her in a very cozy slow dance with some dude whose name she didn't even remember, with the caption, "Looks like former *Good Morning New York* host, Madge Thompson, has found solace in the arms of a new love."

A half hour later she got a text from Jason, "You could have told me the real reason you didn't want to come to Vermont this weekend."

"Fuck, fuck, fuck," she groaned out loud.

23

ANOTHER YEAR'S OVER

December had been a whirlwind of activity in the headlong rush toward the holidays.

The email invitations to The Three Tomatoes' first event in January went out the Monday after Thanksgiving. Trish, Madge, and Suzy had sent it to their contacts, and the Ripe Tomatoes had sent invites to their lists. They had room for one hundred attendees, but were hoping to get fifty for the first event.

The event was titled Life After I Quit, Finding Your Next Act — featuring former *Good Morning New York* host, Madge Thompson, who will be interviewing Tania, Brooklyn's "Grandma Moses."

Madge and Trish were at the gallery bright and early the Tuesday morning after Thanksgiving. Madge was working on the upcoming video interview schedules. Trish was working on details for the event, ordering chairs and deciding on the setup. Then she went online to check out the responses for the event.

"Oh my God! Madge, you're not going to believe this. We just sold out the event."

Madge jumped up and headed over to look at Trish's laptop. "Let me see."

Shaking her head in wonderment, Madge said, "It's not even twenty-four hours since the invite was sent. Let's call Suzy right now."

Suzy was ecstatic too. After work, she headed down to the gallery with a bottle of Dom Perignon.

"Here's to new beginnings," they toasted.

*****

"Don't forgot I have our Ripe Tomatoes holiday dinner tonight," Suzy said as she and Ken headed to the train together. It was unusual for them to be on the same train, since Ken usually took the 7:15 and Suzy usually took a train an hour later. But Ryan had texted late last night and said to get in for an early morning meeting. Suzy was dreading it.

"Well, just think," Ken said after they had miraculously secured two seats together on the packed train, "on December 26 we'll be on our way to Turks and Caicos for a few days of much needed R&R."

"Yes, five more days and counting," Suzy said wistfully.

Suzy grabbed a cappuccino from the Starbucks next door to the agency since their agency "barista" didn't arrive until 8:30 a.m. She had an overwhelming feeling of dread as she headed up in the elevator to her office. She knew the Arpello campaign was failing miserably. And with only three days left to Christmas, it was highly unlikely there would be a sudden surge in sales.

She went straight to the conference room. Their CFO and the head of client talent were already in the room. They exchanged gloomy good mornings and waited for Ryan and Larry, the director of media to arrive.

"This is a fucking disaster," was Ryan's lovely greeting. He slammed a stack of papers on the table just as Larry walked in the room.

"Arpello's marketing director called me last night. They want us to pull all media buys now! The sales are a disaster. And I just got an advanced copy of *Adweek* and they just named our spot the worst perfume ad of the century."

"They'll be short rated," said Larry. "They're better off just running the spots."

"That's what I said," said Ryan, "but the client said they just want the humiliation to end. They're not only firing us, they're pulling the brand off the market."

They all sat there stunned.

"Suzy, why didn't you focus group the goddamned spots?"

Suzy looked at Ryan incredulously. "Focus groups? Ryan, you were the one who was so enamored with the creative and said you knew in your gut it was a winner. And against my advice and better judgment, you said let's present it to the client, no focus groups needed."

Ryan glared at Suzy. "It's your job to make sure the creative delivers on the strategy and to the target audience, and obviously millennials were not relating to this creative."

"Oh really, Ryan? I was the one who told you we should never have targeted the millennial market in the first place. But you wouldn't listen. I wanted to reposition the brand to older women who grew up with it."

"Well, that was a fucking stupid idea then, Suzy, and it's still a fucking stupid idea. If you had put 100 percent into the millennial idea, instead of fighting it, we wouldn't be sitting here now about to fire half of the agency because of your strategic blunder and half-hearted effort."

"My strategic blunder? Ryan, you need to grow up and learn to take responsibility."

Ryan stood there fuming, while everyone in the room sat waiting for the other shoe to drop.

And drop it did. "You know what, Suzy? You're right. I'm taking responsibility right now, and it starts with you. You are fired! I want you out of this office in the next hour."

"You don't have to wait an hour," said Suzy. "I'm out of here now." She glanced over to the head of client talent, and said, "You can ship me my personal belongings." And with that, she was no longer one of the agents of Secret Agent.

***

Well, there's only one thing to do now, thought Suzy as she headed down the subway stairs to the downtown trains. Fifteen minutes later she was walking through the gallery doors.

Trish and Madge both looked up from their laptops. "What are you doing here?" Trish asked, and then quickly added, "Not that you're not welcome and wanted here anytime."

"I just got fired. Let me grab a cup of coffee and I'll give you the gory details."

"That spineless little dick," Madge blurted out after Suzy gave them the blow-by-blow. "So, what are you going to do now?"

Trish added, "Oh, Suzy, I'm so sorry. This must be quite a shock."

"Well, to tell you the truth, this showdown has been coming for quite a while. There have been so many times I would have loved to quit. In fact, Ken kept encouraging me to do that, but we're looking at one hundred and fifty thousand dollars a year in tuition bills for at least the next two to three years. And at my age, I'm a dinosaur in the agency business.

"But the one thing that has really kept me excited, is getting up every morning and thinking about new ideas for The Three Tomatoes. I'd love to be here full-time with both of you and I think we could really accelerate our growth too."

Trish and Madge nodded their heads in enthusiastic agreement. "Oh, Suzy, it would be so great to have all three of us working together here every day," said Trish.

"Well, I have to talk to Ken first and see if we can swing this. But let's get to work. I'm going to draft a press release about our new venture."

Suzy waited until noon to call Ken. She knew he was in meetings all morning.

"Hey, sweetie, what's up?"

Suzy loved hearing Ken's always upbeat voice. She quickly told him what happened.

"Jesus, Suzy, that guy is a real shithead. And you know you have a good case here for age discrimination."

"Maybe, but I don't want to have to go through that kind of humiliation. I just want this chapter of my career to be over," said Suzy.

"Listen," said Ken, "I know you have your Ripe Tomatoes holiday dinner tonight. You should enjoy it. Let's talk this through in the morning. I'll go to the office later tomorrow. I love you and it will all be okay," Ken added assuredly.

24

JUST SAY YES

Trish, Madge, and Suzy slowly made their way uptown in an Uber for dinner with the Ripe Tomatoes. They had all been so busy with various aspects of the upcoming event and official launch of The Three Tomatoes, they'd barely had a chance to talk after Suzy's unexpected arrival and news.

"Listen, I'm not ready yet to tell the Ripe Tomatoes that I got canned," said Suzy.

"Mum's the word," said Trish. "But I am looking forward to some lighthearted holiday cheer. I think we could all use some of that."

"I know this will be a tough holiday for you, Trish. Won't you reconsider spending it with us?" implored Suzy. She knew Madge was heading to Aspen to ski for a few days.

"Thanks, Suzy. But I'll be okay. I just can't face Michael and he's been begging me to spend Christmas with him. And I made excuses to my brother and his wife in Chicago about why we won't be there this year. I'm just not ready to tell them what's happening. My plan is to go to Christmas Eve Mass at St. Patrick's, sleep in Christmas Day, and watch 'It's a Wonderful Life.' I'll be fine, really."

"Well, I leave for Aspen tomorrow," said Madge. She spent every Christmas there skiing with a small group of friends she knew from her early days in journalism. "But I'll be back on the twenty-seventh instead of staying through the new year. We have a lot to do for our event and launch."

"We're here," said Trish. They had just pulled up to the 21 Club in front of the iconic jockey statues. The Ripe Tomatoes loved this spot during the holidays and had reserved a table on the balcony overlooking the main dining room.

Once they were all settled in, Suzy looked around the table at this elegant group of women, beautifully dressed, vibrant, and intelligent. They ranged in age from fifty to nearly eighty, yet not one of them seemed old. They all knew women in this age range and even younger, who were old. *What made this group different?* Suzy thought.

Champagne had been poured, and holiday toasts had been bestowed and they all started to catch up on the latest happenings in their lives.

When asked about the latest on the show, Hope and Celeste shared a sly smile. "Okay, ladies, do not breathe a word of this. It won't be announced until January, but we've signed Joni Evans and Colin McDougal as our leads."

The group buzzed with excitement. This was big news indeed. Joni Evans was an English actress and an Elizabeth Taylor look-alike, much admired for her stage work. She never became a Hollywood star because the juicy film roles always went to Elizabeth. But in the late 1990s she was on a hit TV series that also starred the older, but very debonair Scottish actor, Colin McDougal, who was best known for his recurring role as a spy in one of Hollywood's longest running film franchises. Now, at nearly seventy and eighty years old, their careers were all but over. Or so it had seemed.

Mimi, a Tony Award-winning actress who was one of their Ripe Tomatoes, played a big part in introducing Joni to Hope. She and Joni had been friends for years.

"Joni was reluctant at first, even with Mimi's introduction. But once she met Celeste and realized this was a real story, she was charmed and on board. And Colin's nearly forty-year-younger wife convinced him women would still love to see him on the stage," said Hope. They had already announced shortly after Thanksgiving that three-time Tony Award-winning director, Josh Ellsworth, was coming on board too.

"We have nearly all the money raised, and Catherine Dubois has invited several of her New York City 'ladies who lunch' friends to our first workshop in January. She's convinced when they meet Joni and Colin they'll be in," added Celeste.

"Yes, and with the money almost raised, we're now looking at an April opening date, just in time for the off-Broadway awards season," Hope said excitedly.

Mazel tovs, congratulations, and more glass clinking followed at Hope and Celeste's news.

They went around the table to hear from the rest of the group.

Arlene invited them all to a January fund-raiser fashion show she was putting together for an organization that helps formerly incarcerated women get their lives back. "And the best part," said Arlene, "is the women in the program will be the models. It's amazing how this is helping them build confidence and self-esteem."

Mimi announced that she was opening in a new Broadway show. She was playing Hugh Jackman's mom.

Marilyn had big news too. She was launching a second restaurant with her family's iconic name in Las Vegas. It was opening New Year's Eve.

Listening to their excitement and announcements of new ventures and good causes they were all involved in, Suzy realized the secret to the vitality of these women. It was the power of saying *yes*.

Yes to life and yes to new opportunities. There was no way these "tomatoes" were going into old age wearing invisible cloaks.

The evening was nearly over. They exchanged their Secret Santa gifts and wished each other Merry Christmas and Happy Hanukkah. What would the new year bring their way?

***

Suzy woke up to two of her favorite smells wafting up the staircase — coffee and bacon. She threw on a robe and headed to the kitchen. Ken was dressed in his suit slacks and a striped button-down collar shirt, which he was protecting with a "Kiss the Chef" apron.

"Eggs are almost done," he said as she kissed him on the cheek.

They sat down to Ken's breakfast feast. "Listen, Suzy, I want you to hear me out. I did a lot of thinking last night. You've been absolutely miserable at work for at least the last year. And the only time I've seen you excited is when you're talking about The Three Tomatoes. I think you and Trish and Madge are on to something that has real potential. And you need to give it a real shot. Not just something that you're doing after you've already put in ten hours on a job. You need to go for this now. If you don't you'll always be second-guessing yourself."

"But, Ken, that means not only will I not be bringing home a salary, but I'm going to need to invest in the business too. Madge has already put in fifty thousand dollars and we're going to need another influx of money soon. We've got this house, the kids tuition payments, and..."

"Stop," Ken said emphatically. "Listen, we may have to cut back on a few things, but we can do this. You're never going to get another chance like this, Suzy. You have to go for it now."

"Have I told you lately that I love you? This is the best Christmas present ever," said Suzy as she walked around the table and gave Ken a long passionate kiss.

"Hey, lady, unhand me," laughed Ken. "I have to get to the office. But let's start where this left off tonight."

***

Madge was sitting in first class and sipping a Bloody Mary. She was looking forward to skiing with her old pals, but she couldn't help thinking how her life had changed over the past year. She had no regrets now about leaving the network. It was already starting to feel like another life. The Three Tomatoes chapter was just starting, and she was feeling excited and pumped.

And then there was Jason. How had this man gotten under her skin like this? She had texted him back after Thanksgiving weekend about the now much regretted Page Six photo, and simply said, 'Don't believe everything you see.' She hadn't heard from him since. And she hadn't dared reach out to him. *It's just as well*, she sighed, as she said yes to the flight attendant's offer of another Bloody Mary.

***

It was 6:00 p.m. on Christmas Eve. Trish had never felt so alone. Maybe she should have gone to Suzy's. Well, Midnight Mass might help. Her thoughts were interrupted by the buzz of the apartment intercom. "Yes," she answered.

"There's a Mr. Hogan here to see you," the doorman announced. "Shall I send him up?"

Oh no, thought Trish, *what do I do now?* She had definitely not planned on seeing Michael tonight. What choice did she have now? "Send him up." *It is Christmas and he is still my husband*, she rationalized. She waited anxiously for the doorbell to ring.

And then there he was. "Hi, Trish. I'm sorry to just show up like this, but I knew you wouldn't answer my calls. Can I come in for just a few minutes?" She opened the door to let him in. She took a good long look at him. He looked great. And rested too.

"Listen, Trish. I know I've been an asshole and you don't deserve what I've put you through. But I love you with all of my heart. I'm not asking you to forgive me, but I am hoping that maybe, just maybe you'll spend one last Christmas Eve with me at the apartment, before it's gone for good. I know you said you want to be alone, but we had a lot of good memories there," he pleaded, as a small tear ran down his cheek.

"I...I don't know Michael. I was planning to have a quiet dinner here and then go to Midnight Mass at St. Patrick's," she said half-heartedly as her resolve started failing.

149

"I'll go to Mass with you. And then I'll bring you safely back here. I promise. No pressure. Please, just come back to the old apartment with me."

"Well, I guess no one should be alone on Christmas Eve. Give me a few minutes to get ready."

They walked through the door of their Central Park West building that had been home for the past ten years. They were greeted by Jimmy, the longtime doorman. "So nice to see you, Mrs. Hogan. Merry Christmas." And then they headed up in the elevator.

They walked into the large living room, now empty except for a small couch and a cocktail table. The moving company had loaded up everything the day before. Trish looked around in disbelief. There were tea lights everywhere, and in one corner of the room a Charlie Brown Christmas tree stood with what looked like a picnic blanket in front of it. "Have a seat, I'll be back in one second," said Michael.

She looked out toward the terrace with the twinkling lights of the city for as far as you could see, and she couldn't help feeling melancholy for the life she and Michael had once shared here. Michael was back with two glasses that he filled to the brim with bubbling champagne.

"Merry Christmas, Trish." And they clinked glasses.

"Listen, I have a picnic basket of goodies and I thought we could have a little Christmas picnic under Charlie Brown there."

Trish started to cry. He had recreated their very first Christmas in this apartment. The moving vans were showing up the day after Christmas, but they were so excited about spending Christmas Eve in their new apartment, they had bought a little tree, and had a picnic dinner, right here on the floor.

"Oh, Michael, we did have some wonderful years here," Trish said through her tears.

"Hey," said Michael, gently wiping away her tears, "I wanted this to be a happy Christmas Eve. I'll bring out the food."

They chatted through dinner. Michael wanted to know all about The Three Tomatoes, and this time he was actually listening.

"Trish, I'm really proud of you. And to sell out your first event in a day is an endorsement that you're on to something. And I know you and Madge and Suzy will be unstoppable. I've never know three more determined women.

"I have news too," Michael continued. "I'm starting a job right after the first of the year."

"That's great news," said Trish. "Is it a Wall Street firm?"

"No, actually I'll be going uptown, not downtown for this job. Remember my friend Rob Astor from Goldman Sachs?"

Trish thought for a moment. "Yes of course. He has a lovely wife named Clarissa."

"Yes, that's the guy. He left Goldman Sachs about the same time I did, but instead of staying on the Street, he became a professor at Columbia Business School. We had lunch recently and he told me it was the best move he ever made. He was done with the Wall Street pressure cooker and its empty values. He's never been happier. Says it saved his marriage too. Turns out there was an opening for an adjunct professor in statistics. He recommended me, and I start right after the first of the year. It's a stipend salary, but hey, it's something."

"Michael, that's wonderful. Here's to new beginnings." They clinked champagne glasses again.

They went to Midnight Mass and, as promised, Michael delivered her safely to the door of Madge's apartment. "I'm not going to ask to come in," he said. "But thank you for being with me tonight." And then he pulled a small wrapped package out of his pocket. "Here's a little Christmas present." He kissed her on her cheek and walked away.

Trish sat down and immediately opened the gift. Inside were two brass keys, and a note from Michael.

One of these keys is for you. It's the key to my heart, which you'll have forever. The other key is the key to your heart. I hope someday you'll be able to give it to me. Love forever, Michael.

Trish sat there for a long time, with tears streaming down her cheeks.

25

A NEW YEAR'S JUST BEGUN

It was three days after Christmas. Madge had returned from Aspen the night before, and was raring to get back to work at The Three Tomatoes. Trish was glad to see her back. They caught up briefly on Madge's ski trip. Trish carefully avoided any mention of having seen Michael on Christmas Eve. And they were both excited that Madge would be filming her first "Tomato of Substance" interview with Tania tomorrow morning.

It was a slow time of the year and Madge had been able to get her film crew friends to come down to the gallery. Tania arrived looking absolutely beautiful in a very colorful caftan with a print of Jamaican birds and bougainvillea that her relatives, who were visiting her from Jamaica, had given her for Christmas.

"Tania, I'm glad you were available to do the interview this week," said Madge.

Tania laughed her glorious laugh that sounded like wind chimes, and said, "Oh please. It was a delight to get away from my houseful of guests. And you know what they say about guests and fish."

They all laughed.

Tania was a natural on camera, and Madge was thrilled with the interview. She talked about moving to the housing projects in the Bronx when she was a young teenager, and how her mother insisted she must stay in school. She was the first person in her family to ever go to college. "I loved teaching," Tania said, "but of course in those days, teaching and nursing were about our only options after college. Well, that and marriage."

Tania had never married. She had seen too many good women brought down by no-good men.

"So, Tania, since you retired from teaching you've had two other amazing careers — one in music and one as an artist. Did you feel like you were reinventing yourself?"

"Reinventing myself? Goodness no, child. Why would I want to reinvent myself? I have everything I need inside me. You must keep yourself open to new ideas and new experiences and look inside yourself to find your passions. My passions were music and art. And when you uncover those passions, you evolve. Evolving is the thing that keeps us alive and happy," Tania said with the energy and enthusiasm of a ten-year-old. "We must be ever-evolving."

"Well, that's a wrap," said Madge to the crew. "Tania, that was just perfect. And this is the conversation we'll have with you for our event."

After everyone had left the gallery, Trish and Madge sat back and smiled. "Evolving," said Madge. "That's a much different concept than that phony-baloney reinvention crap we listened to last fall. Tania is the real deal, and she speaks from the heart."

The week was flying by. Suzy had been working on vacation too, and sent them the press release she wanted to send out right after the first of the year. And she had a draft of the first newsletter that would go out to their fledgling database.

And here it was the day before New Year's Eve. Trish and Madge had both been invited to Tania's for a Caribbean-style New Year's Eve party. Madge had begged off. She wanted a quiet night and planned to be asleep before the ball dropped. Trish thought it sounded like fun and accepted Tania's invitation. It was better than spending New Year's pining for Michael and second-guessing herself for not running back into his arms. She needed healing time.

Madge had spent the afternoon at the editing studio of her friends who were finalizing the interview with Tania. "Thanks so much, guys," Madge said. "You really came through for me."

It was a cold day, but the sun was out, and Madge decided to walk home from the Chelsea editing studios to her Murray Hill apartment. Halfway home her phone pinged. It was Jason. "What are you doing tomorrow night? Wanna catch a movie?" She hadn't heard from him since his text on Thanksgiving weekend.

Did he not know tomorrow was New Year's Eve? She texted back, "You mean on New Year's Eve?" He texted back, "Forgot it was NYE. You probably have plans." She thought about that for a minute, and texted back, "Actually I am free, and a movie with a friend sounds perfect."

"Pic u up at 9 PM," he texted back.

***

"Trish, you look beautiful," said Madge. And she did. She was wearing black leggings, a fabulous pair of green velvet Jimmy Choo stilettos, and a long green velvet jacket that showed off her red hair.

"I'm not too overdressed, am I? Tania said dress is festive."

"No, you are perfect. Now shoo...have a wonderful evening."

"Madge, are you sure you don't want to come? I hate leaving you here alone on New Year's," said Trish.

"I'm sure. I'm looking forward to curling up with a good book," Madge replied. And ushered Trish out the door. "Hurry or you'll be late."

Madge hated lying to Trish, but she wasn't ready for another Jason conversation. And now she had less than an hour to get ready. She debated about what to wear. Then decided that casual would be the best option. It was just a movie, not a New Year's Eve date. She threw on a pair of skinny jeans, her suede over-the-knee boots, a red cashmere sweater, and a leather jacket.

She took one quick look at herself when the intercom buzzed. "Mr. Madison is here," said her doorman.

"Tell him I'll be right down."

Jason was dressed in jeans too, so she felt better she had made the right clothing decision. He kissed her on the cheek. "You look great, Madge. I have a car waiting."

They made small talk in the car. How was the farm, how was Chrissy? Did the family all spend Christmas there? And Jason wanted an update on The Three Tomatoes.

"Hey, what theater are we going to anyway?" Madge asked as she realized the car had gone across town and then was heading south.

"We're going to a little theater in Tribeca."

Ten minutes later they were pulling up to the Greenwich Hotel.

"I thought we were going to the movies?" Madge said as Jason led her into the hotel lobby.

"We are. Just follow me." They made a few turns through the lobby and Jason opened the door to the Tribeca Screening Room.

"I rented this just for us for the night," Jason said. "Where would you like to sit?"

Madge was a little confused, but chose two seats near the front of the theater.

"And how about some popcorn and champagne?"

"Well, I'm liking this movie theater, a lot," said Madge. And with that a waiter appeared with two boxes of popcorn and set up a table in the aisle, poured two glasses of champagne for them and returned the bottle to the ice bucket.

"Cheers," said Jason.

"Sir," said the waiter, "are you ready to start the film?"

"We are."

Madge sat back in the recliner chair and waited for the film to begin.

It was the original *Ghostbusters* movie with Bill Murray and Dan Aykroyd. She and Jason were soon laughing out loud. And Jason kept refilling her champagne glass. And before the movie ended they were holding hands too, like a couple of teenagers.

The credits rolled. The lights were still down, when Jason quietly said to her, "Madge, the ghosts are all gone. I want a real, live woman in my life, and that woman is you." And then he leaned over and kissed her gently.

"Jason Madison, you are the most amazing man I've ever met." And with that Madge kissed him back, and this time neither of them wanted to stop.

"Let's take this back to my place," said Jason, and he got no argument from Madge.

***

"Happy New Year, Madge. I am so happy to start this year off with you in my arms." And so was Madge. There was no place she'd rather be than in Jason's bed, snuggled under his armpit. Jason started caressing her body again.

"Wait...I need to send a quick text to Trish. I have a feeling I won't be going home tonight."

They talked and made love throughout the night.

Jason admitted that Madge was right — he been carrying around the ghost of Abigail. "But you were so wrong in thinking I was attracted to you because you are like her. Except for your physical resemblance, you are nothing alike. I did love Abigail. But in retrospect, ours was not a love of equals and it never would have been. She was always going to be my mentor and teacher first. Abigail could only see the boy I had been, not the man I had become.

"Our relationship is nothing like that, Madge. You only know the man I am. And I Iove that you ask for my opinion and advice. I love your tough exterior, and your tenderness inside. And I'm sure one of these days, we'll even get you on a horse. I got you to drive, right?"

They both laughed at that. And fell asleep holding each other tightly. Dreaming of new beginnings.

26

HAPPINESS IS INSIDE US

"I love looking around and seeing you both here," said Trish. It was the second week of the new year. Suzy had returned from vacation and set up her work area in the gallery alongside Trish and Madge.

They had reviewed every detail several times, for this week's launch event. They all agreed it had to be perfect since it was setting the tone and direction for who they are and where they were going.

"I wish we were getting more press to attend the event," bemoaned Suzy. "Of course, Page Six is sending someone, but that's only because they want to find out what Madge is up to. And if Trish is in the poorhouse yet. *The Times* hasn't responded at all. And I've sent invites to some of the big PR firms who handle products for women, but no replies there yet either."

"Yes, but today's *Ad Age* story was great," said Madge. "That might get the attention of advertisers."

The *Ad Age* story headlined with Former Agency Exec and Former News Anchor Launch Website for the Invisible Woman. It picked up most of Suzy's press release, and a reporter had followed up with Suzy for quotes, which gave her a great opportunity to position The Three Tomatoes as a media platform for smart, savvy grownup women.

"Well, let's hope so. And Trish, I'm sorry you barely got a mention in the article," added Suzy.

"I'm very happy to stay low-key right now," said Trish. "And you two are the names that will get us attention."

They had quickly caught up on what was happening in their lives while Suzy was on vacation.

Madge told them about Jason's New Year's Eve surprise.

"Well, that's just about the most romantic gesture I've ever heard of," said Suzy. "So, what happens now?"

"I just want to take it slowly and see where this goes. We still have hurdles, and we're still learning about each other," said Madge. "Although if Jason had his way, we'd both be living on the farm right now. And when I made a reference to *Green Acres* and sang 'Darling I love you, but give me Park Avenue', the age difference reared its ugly head. I looked at Jason's puzzled face and realized he had no idea what I was referring to. Apparently they stopped syndicating the reruns before he was born."

"Well, I know it will all work out," said Trish. She had not mentioned spending Christmas Eve with Michael, but she did tell them that she and Michael had talked and that he had accepted a teaching position at Columbia for the semester.

"It won't help our financial situation much, but I think it's good for Michael's self-esteem."

She had been avoiding Michael's daily phone calls since Christmas Eve. He kept leaving messages begging her to come see the new apartment and talk some more. She finally sent him a text saying she needed space and time. He texted back, "Time is a precious commodity."

This week though, all they had on their minds was the event on Thursday.

"Should we go over the checklist one more time?" Trish asked anxiously.

Madge looked at Suzy, rolled her eyes, and then shrugged. "Okay, Trish, but just one more time. The event will be great."

***

Madge's prediction was right. Women started arriving before 6:00 p.m. The Ripe Tomatoes were all there, and several women had shown up without reservations. Trish didn't want to turn anyone away, and by 7:00 p.m. the gallery could not hold another single body.

Shortly after seven, Trish moved to the front of the gallery where they had set up two high director's chairs for Madge and Tania. She took the microphone to welcome the group.

"I'm Trish Hogan, and welcome to The Three Tomatoes Inspiration and Wellness Center and to our first Three Tomatoes event. This is part of a media platform that I am so grateful to be launching with my two best friends, Suzy Hamilton and Madge Thompson. Together, we are The Three Tomatoes and we're committed to helping each other, and all of you, to live our best lives at every age and every stage of our lives."

Trish's remarks were greeted with enthusiastic applause. Suzy then got up and talked about the "invisible" woman syndrome. "Yet here we are, the most educated, healthiest, and wealthiest women of any generation before us, and we live in a society that tries to marginalize us with their misguided notion of what aging means. Together we will redefine and create a new vision of aging." That was followed by even more enthusiastic applause.

"Tonight's program is titled, "That's *Not* All, Folks," and these two amazing women, our partner Madge Thompson, and the beautiful and ageless Tania, will discuss what that means."

Madge then took the mic. "Some of you may have heard that last fall I quit my job after twenty-five years." That sparked laughter since everyone in the room knew about Madge's highly published departure from the network. "And I'm here to tell you there is life after jumping off a cliff."

Madge held the rapt attention of everyone in the room as she told her story, in much the same way she had told it to Trish and Suzy. Each woman in the room felt a personal connection with Madge as she talked about her feelings leading up to the moment of "I quit", and then her despair at what she had done. She even shared the story of Suzy and Trish breaking into her apartment and finding her sprawled on the couch with an empty bottle of Prosecco and chocolate wrappers strewing the floor.

"So, what have I learned from this besides stocking my fridge with something more than wine and chocolates?" After the laughter, she continued, "Well, I'm still learning. But one of the things I discovered is that I have an identity crisis. You see for years, 'who I was' was totally wrapped up in 'what I did'. I was Madge Thompson, TV journalist. So now I'm trying to figure out who Madge is, and that is still a work in progress.

"But I also had time to be introspective about what I was passionate about doing. And one of those things is bringing people's stories to life in a way that will inspire us all. And tonight, you will hear the story of an amazing woman who keeps evolving."

For the next half hour, Madge interviewed Tania who mesmerized everyone in the room. Her story too was told as if she was sitting across the table with her best friend, enjoying a cup of tea. She had the audience laughing and crying at times.

"You've really led a remarkable life," said Madge.

"Honey, we're all remarkable. All you have to do is keep living, keep breathing, and keep looking inside you for what makes you happy and then do it. Happiness isn't something other people bestow on you. If you're waiting for that, you'll be dead and gone. Everything you need to make you happy is right in here," said Tania as she pointed to her heart.

There were so many questions that Madge finally had to cut them off. "Ladies, ladies, let's enjoy some more wine and I know Tania is happy to talk to you individually."

They also announced their February event, "Menopause Myths, Lies, Truths, and Happiness," and people were clamoring to sign up.

It was after ten o'clock when the last of the crowd left the gallery. The trio had kicked off their shoes and Madge poured them all another glass of wine.

"We did it. Here's to The Three Tomatoes." They all clinked glasses.

"We're going to need a bigger venue for the next event," added Suzy.

27

SURPRISES

Suzy was curled up in a lounge chair by the fireplace in her den. It was a snowy Saturday at the end of January and she was glad for some downtime and a chance to reflect on the progress they had made in the past month.

They had added several new contributors to their website. Arlene had sent two stylists their way who were more than happy to provide style tips with the emphasis on women over forty. Trish, in addition to covering the New York City art scene, had lined up several health experts in nutrition, exercise, and women's health. Mimi and Hope recommended a theater critic and a cabaret reviewer, and they were both on board. As word started to get out about The Three Tomatoes, potential contributors started reaching out to them.

They were ecstatic when one of the top restaurant critics in the country asked if she could become a contributor. Turns out after thirty years of being the restaurant critic at one of New York's iconic magazines, she'd been dropped as a columnist, replaced by a couple of twentysomething food bloggers.

Madge had completed a second interview for their website and YouTube channel. This one was with their designer friend Gabrielle who talked about how being beautiful and sexy has nothing to do with age or size. Gab was going to be on the panel for another one of their events too.

The subscriber base was growing by word of mouth, but they were definitely going to have to do some targeted advertising on social media and hopefully generate some more PR to get the word out.

Her head was swimming with details and resources they were going to need. Not to mention another influx of capital.

She was glad Ian was coming home from college for a quick visit. It would help to get her mind off business, although she was a little concerned about why. He had made it sound like nothing over the phone, "Can't a guy just want to visit his parental units?" he had joked. Well, at least he was taking the train up from Princeton, so she didn't have to worry about him driving on the snowy roads.

***

Ian arrived late in the day, and after their usual banter about school, had headed up to his room until they called him down for dinner. Ken had cleared off the snowy patio to grill steaks, rare just the way Ian liked, and Suzy had made her "world famous" mac and cheese that he loved.

When she realized Ian was basically just moving his food around on his plate, she knew something was wrong.

"Ian, sweetheart, is something going on you want to talk about?"

"Well, actually, Mom and Dad, there is." Then he paused, looking like he wished the floor could open up.

Ken spoke up. "Listen, son, whatever it is you can tell us."

"Emily is pregnant," he blurted out.

Stunned, Suzy stumbled with her words. "Pregnant? How, when?"

Ken chimed in, "Well, we know the how part. I think your mother means how far along is she?"

"It happened over Thanksgiving weekend. We both realized it was a mistake and then we went back to school. We hadn't even talked, and then Emily called me last week to tell me the news. She's telling her parents this weekend too."

They all sat there in silence.

Finally, Suzy asked, "Well, what are Emily's plans? At this stage you know she has options."

"Mom, she's keeping the baby, if that's what you mean. We're not like your generation. And it's my responsibility to man up."

***

It was a beautiful Sunday morning. The sun was out, and the city looked pristine and sparkling covered in a fresh blanket of snow. Although Trish knew soon enough the snowbanks would be covered in yellow dog pee, and then turn to ugly gray slush.

But for now, Trish was enjoying her coffee and the view from Madge's apartment, which she had to herself most weekends now. This weekend, Madge and Jason were in Vermont.

They'd been so busy this month it had been easy to keep thoughts of Michael out of her head — except late at night, when she couldn't sleep and wondered what he was doing. She had texted him last week to see how the teaching was going, and he had simply replied, "Great."

On the top of her dresser she picked up the key to his heart and held it in her palm. She missed Michael and she wasn't at all sure that living separate lives was the way to repair their marriage.

Fifteen minutes later she was dressed and hailing a cab. She'd surprise Michael, see the new apartment, and invite him to breakfast.

The cab slowly made its way up an unplowed Third Avenue to 78th Street. "Just drop me on the corner." She walked halfway down the block to Michael's apartment building and walked into the lobby.

"I'm here to see Michael Hogan," she announced to the doorman.

"And who shall I say is calling?"

"His wife."

He gave her a bit of a strange look as he buzzed Michael's apartment.

"Sorry, he's not answering."

And just as Trish was turning to leave, the lobby elevator opened and out walked Michael arm in arm with Lacey Carter, the lawyer who worked for his former hedge fund.

Trish felt like her feet were cemented to the floor. Michael turned ashen when he saw her, and he immediately walked over to her. "Trish, you should have told me you were coming," he said as he gently tried to take her arm. She recoiled.

And then Lacey sprang into action. "Michael, I'm starving. So nice to see you again, Trish."

Trish ran for the door and around the block, where she promptly threw up at the curb.

***

Madge had called Suzy midafternoon on Monday from Jason's car to check in. "How's everything going? Any new subscribers this weekend?"

"I haven't had a chance to look yet. Trish and I didn't have the best weekends."

"What's going on?"

"We'll tell you tonight. I'll head back to your apartment with Trish later."

Madge arrived home to find Suzy and Trish had already finished a bottle of wine, and had just opened a second bottle. "I leave for one long weekend and the world falls apart," said Madge after hearing both stories.

"So, what's Ian going to do?"

"Well, Emily says she is keeping the baby. She's due in August. After the shock wore off with her parents, they convinced her to finish out the semester, and then come home for the summer to have the baby. That was a relief to us, and we encouraged Ian to finish his semester too."

"What happens after that, who knows? Ian offered to marry her and she said no. But he wants to step up and be a dad to this baby. But God, he's really just a kid. And I can't believe I'm going to be a grandmother."

"And Trish, what a horrible to way to find out about Michael's lover."

"Oh, and that's not the worst of it," said Trish. "I didn't want to tell you this today, Suzy, because you were so upset about Ian, but at noon I got an email from Lacey."

"What did she say?" said an even more shocked Madge.

"She said, 'He doesn't love you, and he hasn't for years. Stay out of our lives.' And five minutes after her email, I got one from Michael, begging me to see him so he can explain. And, telling me how much he still loves me."

"Well that is totally fucked up," said Suzy.

"Yes, it is," said Trish, "but as Scarlett O'Hara would have said, 'I'll think about that tomorrow.' Now let's have another glass of wine."

28

MARCH MADNESS

It was a wind-howling, cold March night that showed no signs of spring being around the corner. Trish, Suzy, and Madge were headed to a Ripe Tomatoes dinner, but first they were stopping for drinks at the cozy little jazz bar at the Kitano Hotel. Tania and her jazz trio were performing there.

They settled into a corner booth and ordered their martinis. Tania had just finished a set and came over to greet them. "Well hello, beautiful ladies." She chatted with them before the next set started.

"You were right, Suzy, to suggest we go out for drinks like old times. We were getting in a rut ending our days at the gallery with a glass of wine," said Madge.

"I agree," said Trish. "And we promised, no shoptalk."

They'd avoided discussing a lot of their personal issues in the gallery lately, just so they could stay focused on work. So, it was good to be out and be girlfriends again.

The martinis arrived. "This is relaxing," said Suzy, as the trio played and Tania sang classic jazz tunes that would have made Ella Fitzgerald proud. "We deserve a break."

They clinked glasses in agreement, and then Suzy asked, "So, Madge, is Jason really going to sell Snazzed?"

"It sure looks that way. If all goes well, they'll close the sale by the end of April."

"And what will Jason do? He's way too young to retire."

"He's not sure yet. But I don't think he'll start another business. He likes to create things, but he never liked the business side of it. He has so many things he's interested in. And he really gets immense pleasure from the simpler things in life, whether it's planting his garden or skiing down a mountain. One of the things he does want to do though is to expand his foundation. We've talked a lot lately about the kind of projects he could support."

"He's so grounded," said Trish. "Even though he was successful at such a young age, he didn't become a jackass like so many of these rich tech guys."

"Well, speaking of jackasses, what's the latest with Michael and the crazy bunny-boiler girlfriend?" asked Suzy.

It had been a rough time for Trish since discovering Michael with Lacey. He had called her nonstop for a week and she finally agreed to meet him for coffee.

He swore he had ended things with Lacey before Christmas. But she wasn't taking no for an answer. She had shown up at his door on New Year's Eve. He told her it was over, and she had to leave. At midnight, he got a call from Bellevue. She had taken an entire bottle of Seconol and then called her doorman just before she passed out. She had listed Michael as her emergency contact.

"I told her she needed help. She started seeing a psychiatrist and she called me a couple of weeks after her suicide attempt to apologize. She said she knew it was over.

"But the night of the snowstorm she showed up at my apartment again. She'd been drinking, and started in about how she couldn't live without me. By then the storm was raging and there was no way I could get a cab or a car to get her home. She basically passed out and 1 let her sleep on the couch. When she woke up the next morning, I told her I'd take her to breakfast. I just wanted her out of the apartment. And that's when we ran into you.

"I walked her to the street and I told her I never wanted to see her again. And I haven't heard from her since then, Trish. I swear to God. I love you and I want you back in my life."

"I'm sorry about this nightmare," said Trish, "but I just can't be part of this craziness right now."

They left the coffee shop together, and hugged each other on the street.

The next day there was an envelope at the gallery door addressed to Trish. When she got inside and opened it, there was a photo of her and Michael hugging on the street. There was huge a red X covering her photo, with a scrawled message that said, "You'll never have him. Die bitch."

That was the day Suzy and Madge urged her to get a restraining order against Lacey.

In answer to Suzy's question, Trish said, "Well, Michael finally got a restraining order against Lacey too this week. He didn't think he needed to until I told him about the photos she was posting to her public Facebook page." She filled them in on the latest.

"She's really a sicko, Trish," said Madge. "To stalk Michael and then take photos when he's not even aware of it and then post them with messages like she took them while she was with him is the sign of an obsessed crazy person. I worry about your safety, Trish, and Michael's too. I wish you'd take Jason up on his offer to hire security for you."

"You know I appreciate the offer, Madge, but hopefully with Michael's restraining order this will end."

"Let's hope so," said Suzy. But silently she and Madge both worried.

***

"Your first two events were really special," said Celeste after everyone had settled in for dinner. "You've created something wonderful for all of us." All the Ripe Tomatoes agreed.

"And what's the latest with the play?" asked Suzy.

"It's the usual preopening jitters right about now. But it's going really well," said Hope, "despite what you may have read in the gossip columns." Hope was referring to a nasty column in one of the daily papers about tension on the set, and conflict with Joni and Colin. And then the columnist added the ultimate insult, that "Industry insiders question whether theatergoers will buy tickets to a romantic story about aging seniors portrayed by fading stars."

"I'd bet money Ellen Martin's feeding these rumors to her favorite columnist. It's a shame because the truth is it's such a delight to work with real pros. Joni Evans and Colin McDougal are a joy. It sure beats working with all those spoiled movie stars who want to do 'theater', but have had no training. And I can't believe we actually open the first week in April. You'll all be there, right?"

There were yeses all around the table and Mimi added, "I'll be there with bells on, and my best finery. My stand-in is taking over for me in my show because I wouldn't miss this opening." This was no small gesture since Mimi was a lead in a smash hit Broadway musical.

"Mimi, if it wasn't for you we wouldn't have Joni and Colin," said Hope.

"I'm just so happy to have Joni in New York for a while. Even though we're both crazy busy with our shows, we have dinner together every Sunday night."

"Well, Celeste and I really appreciate the support of all of you," said Hope. "And by the way, Ellen just posted on her 'Ellen's fabulous life' Facebook page, that she has moved up the opening of her new show to April. She had a photo of herself posing in front of the theater with the poster in the background. Honestly, I don't know how that bitch has time to produce since she's always posing somewhere and posting photos of herself to Facebook. Anyway, it looks like she rushed to open her show to make the cutoff date for the Obies. We may just be going head-to-head this year."

The conversation continued to buzz with show biz gossip. Trish, who was sitting next to Arlene, had noticed she was unusually quiet. She leaned in and whispered, "Are you okay?" With that Arlene started to cry. Within moments the table was silent. They were all shocked to see Arlene's perfect facade start to crumble.

Trish put an arm around Arlene, and assured her whatever it was, she could tell them.

Arlene finally pulled herself together, and said, "Harry has been diagnosed with Alzheimer's."

They all gasped, because Arlene had not breathed a word to anyone, which was not unusual considering how closed she always was about her personal life.

"It's been going on for months. At first, I thought it was just forgetfulness, and senior moments. But then he couldn't remember what floor we live on. And last week the doorman found him aimlessly walking around the lobby. I don't know what I'm going to do." She dissolved into another round of tears.

Celeste spoke first. "Listen, Arlene, you are not alone in this. We are all here for you and will help in any way we can."

Suzy looked around the table at the love and genuine concern and knew they all would be there for Arlene, and each other. Even with her worries about Ian and Trish too, she went to sleep that night feeling blessed that she had these wonderful women in her life.

.

29

APRIL SHOWERS

Trish started off their weekly Friday morning status meeting. "I'd like us to revisit my initial concept for the gallery to become a women's inspiration and wellness center. Now that we've got the monthly events running smoothly and the theater down the street to hold them in, here's my idea."

Madge and Suzy listened to Trish's thoughtful presentation. First, they'd put French doors toward the rear of the gallery to close off the office area they had created for themselves. The rest of the gallery could be used for workshops during the week and on weekends too. Trish had a good lineup of experts in health and wellness who could lead workshops, as well as career and life coaches too who could help women get to their "next." It could also be a source of income for The Three Tomatoes.

"Let's do it," said Suzy, "but under one condition."

"And what would that be?"

"That the income from the workshops is yours," said Suzy, and Madge agreed.

Trish vehemently rejected that plan. "Listen, you've both put in seed money to get us going, and neither of you are taking money out. I need to be able to make my fair contribution too, and this is one way I can do that."

Madge pointed out, that first, it had been Trish's idea that led to The Three Tomatoes, and that had great value. And second, they had rent-free offices at the gallery.

"All right," Trish finally acquiesced. "Thank you both, and I really could use the income."

Madge was excited that their video series, *Women of Substance*, was doing well in terms of views, and it was helping drive traffic to The Three Tomatoes website.

"Well, that brings us to the chicken and the egg conundrum," said Suzy. "We need more subscribers to attract advertisers and sponsors, and we need advertiser and sponsor dollars to cover marketing costs to acquire more subscribers. But that's just part of the issue. We still have to convince marketers why this demographic should be important to them.

"It's frustrating as hell. Yesterday I sat in the offices of one of the top PR firms in New York City that represents some of the biggest companies in beauty and cosmetics in the world. In the past month alone, they have launched six antiaging products clearly aimed at our demographic. But when we talked about sponsorships, the president said that while the products are for our demographic, the client's marketing teams prefer that they be advertised in media that targets women under forty-five."

"That just makes no sense," said Trish. "And when did aging become an 'anti', like it's a disease."

"I agree," said Suzy. "But it's the same thing I went through with Arpello. The client marketing teams and the agency media buyers are not at all interested in marketing to 'old' people who they think do not try new brands. And they also think if they market to an older audience, even if the product is geared to them, the product will get stigmatized as just for 'old' people. We need a brave marketer who is willing to change the tide."

"Well, no one said this was going to be easy," Madge reminded them. "We knew this would be an uphill battle, but we're The Three Tomatoes. We will not surrender, and we will not be invisible. We will wear our Jimmy Choos, our miniskirts, and dye our hair any damn color we choose, and screw the notion of what's age appropriate. We will not let the bastards win." They both laughed at Madge's rousing pep talk.

***

By midafternoon, Trish had outlined a series of workshops and started to contact potential workshop leaders. At the top of her list was a workshop for women, like Arlene, who were taking care of loved ones with dementia or serious illness. Since Arlene's revelation about her husband's Alzheimer's diagnosis, Trish had reached out to her with resources and moral support.

Madge was writing her weekly blog for The Three Tomatoes, "That's *Not* All, Folks", which was becoming very popular with their subscribers. She highlighted some of the women she was interviewing, but also added her very humorous and self-deprecating thoughts on aging. The blogs were being shared by other bloggers too.

Suzy's cell phone rang, and she walked to the other side of the gallery to take the call so she wouldn't disturb Trish and Madge.

Ten minutes later she walked back to their office area, ecstatic. "You know that thing you always tell us, Trish, about putting your wishes out to the universe? Not that I've ever really believed that, but I may now."

"What are you talking about?" asked Madge.

"That call, ladies, was from Margot Tuttinger's assistant. Margot wants to meet with me first thing Monday morning to see if The Three Tomatoes would like to consult with her on a second launch of Arpello, but this time using my idea of a retro brand marketed to women over forty-five. We may just have found our brave marketer."

"Now that's the way to end the week," said Trish.

***

A couple of hours later, Trish walked into Madge's apartment, kicked off her shoes and poured herself a glass of wine. Madge was spending the weekend with Jason at his loft in the city. It was times like this when she really missed Michael. There was no one to share details of her week with and she had no plans for the weekend. It was a loneliness that felt like she had a hole in her center. One of the reasons she wanted to start the weekend workshops was to keep her mind off Michael, not to mention crazy Lacey.

There had been no threats or evil notes since the restraining order, but Trish realized she hadn't looked at Lacey's Facebook page in a while. The thought of it made her sick, but her lawyer had suggested she monitor social media too.

She refilled her glass of wine and opened up the Facebook app on her phone to Lacey's page. She almost dropped her glass. There were several new postings. The first was a picture of Lacey getting out of a bathtub wearing Michael's initialed bathrobe — the one Trish had given him the Christmas before last. It was captioned, "Want to join us, Trixie?" The second was a photo of the eighteenth-century antique armoire that Michael had kept for the apartment.

One drawer was open revealing frilly lingerie, with the caption, "Move over, Trixie."

Before she could even think about it, she was calling Michael. He answered right away. "Trish, it's..."

She didn't wait for his greeting. "You bastard," she screamed into the phone. "You're seeing her again. How could you? And now she's threatening me again."

"Trish, calm down. What the hell are you talking about? I haven't seen Lacey since the January fiasco."

"Pull up her Facebook page right now, and then tell me you're still not seeing her."

Trish waited. And then Michael came back on the phone. His voice was quivering, "Trish, I swear I don't know anything about these photos, and I am not seeing her."

"Then how the hell is she in your robe and how does she have a drawer in our armoire filled with her lingerie?"

"I have no idea, Trish...unless...oh my God...unless she somehow got a key to the apartment. I'm calling the police right now. Trish, please be careful, this woman is nuts."

Trish was trembling. She hung up on Michael, and called Suzy and told her what happened.

"Trish, you are coming to our house and staying here tonight. And first thing in the morning I am going with you to the police. You need to report this too."

As they were leaving the police station the next morning, Suzy turned to Trish and said, "I am just appalled. Even though you have a restraining order, and she is clearly threatening you, their hands are tied?"

"I know. I can't believe he said, well there's no way to prove 'Trixie' is meant for you, and we have no way of knowing that your husband didn't invite her to his apartment. And Michael didn't fare much better last night. The police asked him if he had ever invited Lacey to his apartment. And when he said yes, they said there's no way to prove she didn't take those photos then. At least he's changed the locks and alerted the building to block Lacey from entering. But who knows, maybe Michael is lying to me."

"Well, either way it's scary. And I hate seeing you go through this kind of hell. Come back to the house and we'll do something fun to take our minds off this."

By Sunday afternoon, Trish was much more relaxed and insisted on heading back into the city. "Hey, you've got a big day tomorrow," she said to Suzy. "You need your beauty sleep."

***

Suzy took a deep breath as she pressed the elevator button to the penthouse office of Margot Tuttinger. She was immediately escorted into a beautifully appointed office with a glass desk, antique rugs, and floor-to-ceiling glass windows with drop-dead views of the city.

"Suzy, have a seat. It's lovely to see you again. I must say, I was pleased to hear you left that horrid little agency, and I'm very excited about your new venture. So, let's talk about how the consulting arm of The Three Tomatoes might help with raising Arpello from the dead. I know we should just let it go, but the brand is very special to me. You see, I was the brand manager for the original Arpello."

Suzy didn't mention that she knew that, nor did she mention she knew Jason. She and Margot talked for the next hour. Suzy agreed that a second relaunch would be a bit dicey, and not something that too many brands had successfully done. But, if they handled it carefully, it was possible. She outlined her approach, including focus groups with women who remembered the brand. At the end of the hour, Margot had offered The Three Tomatoes a very generous six-figure consulting fee. She couldn't wait to get back to the gallery and share the news with Madge and Trish.

***

The next couple of weeks were uneventful. There had been no new postings on Lacey's social media pages and Trish was breathing a little easier. She was looking forward to the first workshop this weekend too. And they were all looking forward to tonight's opening of Hope and Celeste's play.

The Ripe Tomatoes were all gathered in the lobby of one of the largest off-Broadway theaters in Times Square. Everyone looked fabulous as usual. And they were all glad that Arlene had made it there too. Caring for her husband was becoming increasingly difficult.

Mimi said, "I feel as nervous as if it's my own opening night." They all agreed they had jitters, and then made their way to their seats.

Hope was backstage, pacing like a panther. She kept peering out into the audience and was calmed a bit by the reassuring sight of the Ripe Tomatoes. No matter what, she knew they'd be there for her.

She turned to Celeste, who was waiting in the wings too, took her hands, and said, "Let's break a leg."

The curtain opened, and the applause was deafening when Joni Evans stepped on the stage as Celeste and walked into the rabbi's office. And when Colin McDougal appeared for his first date with Celeste, there was a standing ovation for both of them.

The Ripe Tomatoes laughed out loud, as did the rest of the audience, at the scene where Celeste tells them at dinner about her new boyfriend.

The score was beautiful, a combination of classics from *The American Songbook* and new tunes written for the show. There wasn't a dry eye at the end of the show, which was followed by a ten-minute, standing ovation for the brilliant stars.

Hope had stayed behind in the theater, to catch her breath. "I'll meet you all at Sardi's," she said to Celeste and the cast. Now she was just praying that the critics would love the show as much as the audience did.

She had touched up her hair and lipstick and headed out the backstage door where her car would be waiting. She stopped short. Standing there, with a fabulous bouquet of flowers, was Marvin.

"Hope, I just wanted to tell you the show was wonderful. I'm so glad I got to see it on opening night. I knew you could do it, and I'm so proud of you."

Hope stood there, speechless for a moment, and then said, "Oh, Marvin, you are the kindest man I've ever known. Come on, you're coming to Sardi's with me."

He protested that he wasn't wearing a tux, but Hope said he looked absolutely wonderful just the way he was.

When Hope walked into the upstairs private room at Sardi's on Marvin's arm, the Ripe Tomatoes looked at each other and smiled, especially Mimi who had a ticket delivered to him one night when he was bartending at the New York Athletic Club.

When the reviews came in the next day, the critics loved the show as much as the audience. It would be a shoo-in for nominations.

30

THE MERRY MONTH OF MAY

It was the first weekend in May and the snow had finally melted in Vermont. It was a beautiful Saturday night and the sky was crystal clear. Jason had made a fire in the pit, and he and Madge were enjoying a glass of brandy.

"You know, I never realized there were so many stars in the sky," said Madge. "The bright lights of New York City dim them. Oh, and look, there goes a shooting star," she added in wonderment.

"Well, now you're starting to get what I love about being here, City Girl."

"Now that you've sold Snazzed, there's nothing stopping you from living here full-time."

Jason just looked at her for a long moment. "Nothing? Really, Madge? When are you going to stop treating us like a casual relationship?"

"That's not what I meant, Jason. You know I can't leave the city, and I don't want you to feel you need to stay there, when you'd rather be here."

"I'd rather be where you are, Madge, and that's the difference between us. It's like the difference between can't and won't."

"Jason, you know I'm committed to making The Three Tomatoes successful. It's important to me, not to mention my two best friends. And you of all people should know the time that has to be invested to make a new venture work."

"I do, Madge. And it also takes resources, which is why you really need to let me infuse the capital you need into the business. No strings attached. It's a gift."

"We do need capital. But first I'd have to convince Suzy and Trish. And second, there is no way this could be a gift. You'd be an investor."

"Well, I do have an ulterior motive, you know. The sooner you make The Three Tomatoes successful, the sooner you might consider a real life with me. Think about it, Madge. We could do anything and go anywhere."

"Jason, you promised no pressure. Now seriously, what are you going to do now?"

"I really want to focus on my foundation and I'd like your help to identify what we could do to make the most impact. You've traveled the world and done so many stories on people who need help. I've been thinking a lot lately that our focus should be on women and girls. I think men have done a piss-poor job of running the planet. And after going from doctor to doctor with Abigail, I think we need a health care system that puts women's health at the forefront too."

"I'd love to help with ideas. You know there are a lot of great organizations on the ground that are doing wonderful work, but are very underfunded. I could start drawing up a list for you. And Trish is a great resource for women's health. I know she'd have some thoughts on that."

"Great. And now that you've steered the conversation away from us, which you are so good at doing, you never answered my question last night about meeting my parents."

Madge sighed. "It's not that I don't want to meet them, Jason. I just feel awkward. I mean, your mother's not that much older than me."

"Madge, my parents aren't like that. They certainly never judged Abigail, and they would have had a lot more reason to be upset about that relationship, since I was barely out of college, than ours."

"I just can't yet."

"Fine. Let's go in. It just got very chilly out here.

***

Suzy was looking forward to sleeping in on Saturday morning. When her phone rang at 6:00 a.m. she immediately panicked. No one calls this early unless it's bad news.

"Suzy, it's Hope."

"Hope, what are you doing up at this ungodly hour? Is something wrong?"

"No, everything is right. We did it. We just got nominated for an Obie and word has it we'll be nominated for the Drama Desk and all the other off-Broadway show awards too."

"Oh, that's wonderful news. Worth being awakened for."

"And get this...Ellen's new musical has been nominated too, so we'll be going head-to-head with the evil bitch."

"Well, if the Obie voters have any good sense, *If Tomorrow Never Comes* is a sure winner. And now that I'm awake, how are things going with Marvin?"

Hope giggled. "Quite well actually. He's licking my toes right now. Gotta go."

Ken was awake now too. "I gather Hope's show got nominated?"

"Yes, and I'm delighted for her and Celeste. Although I wish she could have held off her news for a couple of more hours."

Ken had moved closer. "Well, since you're awake," he said kissing her.

A short while later they were snuggled in each other's arms. "You know I had forgotten how nice morning sex is," said Suzy, before she fell back to sleep.

***

Madge waited until the end of the day on Monday to talk to Suzy and Trish about Jason's proposal.

They had just poured wine when Madge told them that Jason was willing to put two million dollars into The Three Tomatoes.

"Two million dollars?" said Suzy incredulously.

Trish was too stunned to speak.

"Yes. And he wanted to do it as a gift, but I told him if we all agree, he'd have to be an investor. Just think what this could do for us though. We could get to our three-year projections in the next year with this kind of boost, not to mention we'd get salaries too."

Excitedly, they pulled out their business plan.

"Well, with that kind of money, we could do a real advertising campaign. We could also hire an editor, a full-time web person, and a couple of young people to do all our social media," said Suzy.

An hour later they had made the decision to let Jason invest in their company.

And when Madge told them about the foundation and the women's health idea, Trish had a ton of ideas for that too.

"Let me call Jason and tell him the news that's he's now Mr. Tomato."

She returned a couple of minutes later. "Jason is thrilled, and he just invited us to the loft for champagne and dinner. He's cooking."

***

Over the next two weeks Suzy, Trish, and Madge mapped out their immediate needs and divided up the next steps for The Three Tomatoes.

Suzy made an offer to Amy, the digital creative director from her former agency, to join them as their webmaster. Amy was thrilled, and turned in her resignation to Suzy's old boss, Ryan, that afternoon. Suzy had to admit she enjoyed Amy's recounting of Ryan's meltdown when Amy told him where she was going. "And by the way," said Amy, "when Kathy heard I was joining you, she said to tell you if you need a social media maven, she'd love to be considered." By the end of the week, Kathy had joined The Three Tomatoes too.

Arlene had recommended a couple of "tomato" editors who had been laid off in the shrinking magazine business, and Trish had agreed to interview them.

Now that they were adding staff, they realized the gallery wasn't going to work much longer for workshops and their offices. When

Jason offered them the office space at the loft that was now vacated since the sale of Snazzed, they jumped on it.

And here they were, two weeks later, eating lunch in the loft conference room.

"This is so weird," said Madge. "Just a few months ago I was interviewing Jason right at this table. I could never have imagined all that's transpired since then to bring me back to this very table."

"A lot has changed for all of us since then," said Trish, with that sad look in her eyes that never quite went away. Then she immediately added, "Oh, I'm sorry how that just sounded. It was a momentary pity party, which is ridiculous since I have so many good things to celebrate."

"Trish, if anyone is entitled to a pity party it's you. You don't have to feel like you need to always put on a happy face with us," said Suzy.

"I know," said Trish. "And I love you both for that. I have this part of my life that's one of the most exciting things that's ever happened and then the other part of my life that's been the most difficult. Thank goodness I have this part."

"Yep," said Suzy. "And we have the Obie Awards to look forward to tonight too. I'm so excited for Hope and Celeste."

***

"And the winner of the best new American theater work is..." the presenter paused as everyone held their breath "...If Tomorrow Never Comes."

The Ripe Tomatoes leaped out of their seats and joined the chorus of applause throughout the theater. Suzy couldn't help looking over at Ellen Martin and her entourage who were half-heartedly applauding and had remained in their seats.

An ebullient Hope made a dramatic entrance across the stage, in a royal blue satin cocktail dress, her hair swept up to show off the long rhinestone earrings dangling from her ears. Joining her from the other side of the stage was Celeste, in a classic black Chanel cocktail dress that showed off her size six frame and great legs.

Both were in tears as they accepted the award, as were every one of the Ripe Tomatoes.

Ellen Martin made a brief appearance at the after-party, and before leaving on her broom, made her way to the throng of people congratulating Hope and Celeste. "Hope, so excited you *finally* won an award."

Ellen's entourage, not ones to leave a "see and be seen" party, stayed on and one by one made their way to Hope with effusive congratulations and invitations to lunches and cocktails.

Hope leaned over to Suzy and said, "Success really is the best revenge."

31

NOSTALGIA

"Margot will be here in an hour," said Suzy. "I'm so nervous you'd think this is my first client presentation. My palms are sweating."

"Suzy, the presentation is brilliant," said Trish. "And, Madge, the video interviews are compelling."

Suzy had conducted focus groups with women over forty-five who remembered Arpello from their youth. She had conducted groups in New York, Chicago, and L.A. Over and over, the women talked about how they associated Arpello with their "firsts" — first kiss, first love, first lover. And they all talked about the dreamy guy in the ads they were in love with. Their positive emotions with the brand were intertwined with the dreamy guy.

Suzy then had the idea of having Madge interview six of these women who had best articulated their feelings about the brand, and getting those interviews on film. The edited video was a love letter to Arpello and the Arpello guy.

Margot had shown up precisely on time, with no staff. After the humiliating relaunch effort during the holidays, she was keeping a possible relaunch completely under the radar and away from her marketing teams. She blamed herself for paying too little attention to the last launch and ignoring her gut, which had always been her North Star. She was not about to let that happen this time.

"I admire what you're doing," Margo said after Suzy introduced Trish and Madge. "I spent many years in France where older women are revered for their intelligence, style, and sophistication. And while I admire the beauty of youth, I've never understood why we Americans worship at its feet. So, Suzy, what have you discovered?"

Suzy spent the next hour discussing the research, the focus groups, and the psychology of the emotional connection of Arpello's fans.

"The nostalgia for Arpello that we heard in every focus group is not at all surprising," said Suzy. "I spoke with two leading consumer behavior psychologists who talked about how our early years are key to our psychological development. These women formed an enduring aesthetic preference for Arpello during the sensitive period of their late adolescent and early adulthood and, as you will see when asked to recall Arpello, they have maintained this early preference."

She then showed the video interviews where all six women lovingly recalled their emotional relationship to Arpello.

"We were so inspired by these women, that we took the liberty of coming up with a creative concept. I know that is not what you hired us to do, but we'd like to share it with you."

"Please," said Margot, not showing any emotion.

With that Suzy unveiled a large poster that was on an easel in front of the room. They had convinced Jason to pose for a photo session just the way his father had thirty-five years ago, in a white open-collar shirt, with a few buttons open exposing his chest. The copy said, "Remember your first time? Arpello...timeless."

Margot sat there in a three-minute silence that felt like the slow drip, drip, drip of a faucet. And then finally, she said, "Well-done, ladies. But you've made one mistake."

Flustered, Suzy said "And what would that be?"

"Well, as much as I adore Jason, and he certainly looks like his father at that age, his father should be the face of the relaunch. And let me tell you, John is as sexy at sixty-five as he was at twenty-five."

Of course, thought Suzy. *This is why Margot Tuttinger is the powerhouse she is.*

"Margot, you are absolutely right. I don't know why we didn't think of that. Do you think he'd do it again?"

"There's only one to find out. We'll just have to ask. And where is Jason? He promised me champagne on the terrace."

"Madge, do you want to let Jason know we're heading up?" said Suzy trying to stay cucumber cool when her brain was saying *we did it*.

As they headed up the stairs, Margot said to Madge, "I'm looking forward to getting to know you, Madge. You've brought Jason back to life."

***

"So, you've rejected me as the face of Arpello," said Jason laughing. "And what makes you think you'll get my father to say yes again, Aunt Margot?"

"Actually, I was thinking we could enlist Suzy, Madge, and Trish to help with that. After all, they've convinced me to do a second relaunch of the brand."

Jason looked at Madge, thought for a moment, and then said, "Madge and I were heading up to the farm for Memorial Day weekend. My parents haven't been to the farm in a while. I could invite them. Why don't you join us, Aunt Margot, and you too, Suzy and Trish? It would be a nice chance for my parents to meet all of you."

"Well, that's one way to corner him," said Margot. "I'd love to join you."

"I'll talk to Ken," said Suzy. "We don't have any plans and that sounds great."

"Well, I wish I could join you," said Trish, "but I have a workshop on Saturday. But I think your father won't stand a chance with this group."

***

After Suzy, Trish, and Margot left, Jason turned to Madge. "Listen, I'm sorry. I know I sabotaged you into meeting my parents. I shouldn't have done that." He looked like a guilty ten-year-old.

"No, you shouldn't have, Jason. But I shouldn't have been such a jerk about not wanting to meet your parents. And it will be easier having Suzy and Margot there."

"So, I'm forgiven?" said Jason moving in closer to Madge, and kissing her neck.

"Come here, you sexy man."

32

BACK AT THE FARM

Madge had been fussing with the place settings for twenty minutes to make sure they were perfect. Everyone, including Jason's parents, was expected to arrive in time for lunch.

Jason came up behind her and put his arms around her waist and gave her a kiss on her neck. "Sweetheart, my parents will love you."

"Well, my stomach is doing flip-flops. I can't remember when I felt this nervous."

The cowbell clanged at the front porch, and Madge jumped. "I'll get it," said Jason heading to the front door.

And soon she heard the welcoming sounds of Suzy's and Ken's voices. Madge joined them in the hallway. "Oh, thank God you're both here first."

Jason helped them with their luggage and showed them to their room upstairs.

They quickly rejoined Madge downstairs. "I'll unpack later," said Suzy. "You look like you need backup."

Madge escorted them to the porch off the kitchen, where she had a couple of bottles of champagne chilling in a bucket.

"Well, here's to friendships and the start of a wonderful weekend," said Jason as they toasted.

"I hope you're saving some of that for us," a deep male voice boomed from the kitchen.

"Mom, Dad, we didn't hear you come in," Jason said as he immediately embraced his parents. "Let me introduce you to everyone."

Madge went to put her hand out, but was immediately embraced in a bear hug by Jason's dad, John. When he released her, Elizabeth, Jason's mom, grabbed Madge's hands and held them tightly. "Oh, Madge, we are so happy to meet you, and even happier that Jason met you." She then gave Madge a kiss on the cheek.

Introductions were made all around and within fifteen minutes, everyone was at ease, thanks to Jason's charming and gracious parents.

Suzy and Madge were having a hard time taking their eyes off John. Just as Margot had said, the man still oozed sex appeal.

Madge couldn't help thinking this is how Jason will look one day too, when his dark hair turns to silver. And now looking at Elizabeth, Madge knew where Chrissy got her blond hair, blue eyes, and graceful frame. Jason and Chrissy hit the lottery on the gene pool. And while Jason looked like his dad, his wonderful smile was definitely a gift from his mother.

In the distance, they could see Chrissy rounding the horse stables and when she spotted her parents she rushed to join them on the porch and there were more hugs all around. The cowbell rang again, and within moments Jason was escorting Margot out onto the porch, where she and Elizabeth greeted each other like giddy teenagers.

After lunch, Jason took his dad and Ken for a tour of the farm. Chrissy excused herself to check on one of her pregnant mares. Madge, Suzy, Margot, and Elizabeth had returned to the back porch to enjoy another glass of wine.

"Lunch was wonderful, Madge," said Elizabeth.

"I can't take any credit. That was all Bertha's doing," said Madge. "I just set the table."

"Well, lunch was wonderful because of the company. It wouldn't have mattered what we ate," Elizabeth said graciously. "So, Margot, what are you up to these days?"

"I am so glad you asked," said Margot. "And actually, we need to enlist your help. I've been working with Suzy and Madge to help relaunch Arpello."

Margot filled Elizabeth in on all the details, and what the research was showing them.

"So, you see, Elizabeth, having John as the face of Arpello again is critical to our relaunch success. Will you help us convince him?"

Elizabeth smiled that awesome Jason-like smile, and said, "I love the idea. But it might be more difficult to convince John this time around than it was forty years ago. But I think if the four us conspire he won't stand a chance." They soon hatched a plan.

Just before dinner was served, Madge whispered to Jason, "After dinner invite everyone into the living room for after-dinner drinks, not to the fire pit."

Hmmm, thought Jason, *wonder what that's all about.*

Dinner was a joyous affair and the conversation sparkled as they all got to know each other better.

"That was a delicious dinner," said Ken. "And thank you, Jason, for the tour of the farm. I see why you love it here so much."

"And I'll have to run around all two hundred acres tomorrow to burn off just a few of the calories I consumed," laughed John.

"Well, why don't you all head into the living room. Dad, there's brandy and port if you want to do the honors, while Madge and I clean up the kitchen," said Jason.

Everyone wanted to help with cleanup, but Madge and Jason insisted they could handle it just fine.

Madge was bending over the dishwasher when Jason came up in back of her. "Now that is just about the most perfect derriere in the universe." Madge stood up and Jason embraced her. "See I told you, you had nothing to worry about. My parents adore you."

"And I think they are just wonderful, and now I know why you and Chrissy are the awesome people you are."

"So, what's the plot, Madge? Why didn't you want us to enjoy brandies by the fire pit?"

"All will be revealed shortly," Madge laughed with a twinkle in her eyes.

With the kitchen cleaned up, Jason and Madge returned to the warm and cozy living room. There was a roaring fire, and everyone was enjoying their brandies and port. John was telling Suzy and Ken how he first met Margot and Elizabeth at an off-campus party at Harvard. He was with a date, but the second he spotted Elizabeth he felt like he had been struck by a thunderbolt.

"I spent the entire semester pursuing her until she finally agreed to go out on a date with me. But that was only after I convinced

Margot that I wasn't another Harvard playboy, and she convinced Elizabeth to say yes. So, I really had to court them both."

"Well, dear, you know Margot can convince anyone to do anything. But the truth is I didn't really need convincing. You were the best-looking guy I had ever seen and that made me nervous," said Elizabeth. "And you're still the best-looking guy too."

"Oh, flattery will get you anything," said John.

"Well, I hope so dear, because actually we have a proposal for you. But we want to show you something first." And with that, Suzy picked up the TV remote, hit Play, and there was the first of the women Madge had interviewed talking about the Arpello guy.

When the video ended, Margot told John about the relaunch plans. "And the only way this has a chance of succeeding is if you agree to be the face of Arpello again."

John sat there stunned. "I didn't want to do that when I was twenty-five. And I certainly don't want to do this at sixty-five. I'm an old man. I'll look ridiculous."

For the next hour, Suzy, Madge, Margot, and Elizabeth talked John through the research, the brand strategy, and why he would be perfect for the relaunch.

"So, Jason, is this why you invited us here this weekend? I thought it was to finally meet Madge. But now I see it was a grand conspiracy." He looked at them all furiously for a minute. Then he started laughing. "Damn, I didn't stand a chance, did I? And forty years ago, it was just two strong persuasive women, now it's four."

"So, is that a yes?"

"Damn it, Margot, yes."

***

They all awoke to the smells of coffee and bacon on a perfect Sunday morning. Gradually, everyone made their way to the kitchen where Jason whipped up individual omelets for everyone. After breakfast, Elizabeth asked if anyone would like to join her for a walk.

"Oh, I'd love to," Madge said right away. Suzy and Margot glanced at each other and each begged off.

As they walked, Elizabeth talked about how much Jason loved the farm. "From the time he was a little boy, he'd follow his grandfather around this place. And every summer it was the only place he ever wanted to be. John never had the same feeling for it, which is why we sold it when his father died. And it had fallen into such disrepair that we weren't at all sure that Jason had made the right decision in buying it back. But oh my, look at it now. His grandfather would be so proud."

"Well, you know, I've been a city girl all my life," said Madge, "but being here is restorative. It took me a while, but I understand now why Jason loves being here."

"Let's sit by the pond a minute," suggested Elizabeth. And they both sat on the little wrought-iron settee.

"Madge, I know from Jason that you thought we would be judging you. Or comparing you to Abigail. And I have to be honest. As a mother, I want to know that the woman my son loves with all his heart is going to love him with all of her heart. And, Madge, that is what I see when I look at you and Jason together. I know that you have made him happier than I have ever seen him. And I think he has made you happy too. And really, that's all you can ask for in life — to love and be loved with all your heart. That will take you the distance, my dear."

Madge found herself tearing up. "Thank you for saying that, Elizabeth. I have never loved anyone like I love Jason. He's made me a better person. And I have to thank you and John for raising such an extraordinary human being."

Now Elizabeth had teared up too. They hugged, and Elizabeth said, "Well, let's head back. Chrissy is determined to get us all on horses today."

They headed back to the barn where Chrissy had saddled up the horses. "Okay, city folks. We're going on an easy trail ride, and I promise you'll enjoy it. And don't look so scared, Madge and Suzy. I've got you on two of our most gentle horses. They're the ones I take the young schoolkids on."

Chrissy guided them along a beautiful trail through the woods and then to the top of one the smaller mountains, where they rested and reveled in the view of the farm below and the mountains around then.

When they returned to the barn midafternoon, Suzy and Madge were exhilarated.

"Chrissy that was a wonderful time," Madge said as Cecil, her horse, nestled his head on her shoulder. "I think I'm in love."

"Oh, so I have competition?" laughed Jason.

As they made their way back to the house, Suzy's cell phone rang. "It's Trish, she's probably missing that she couldn't join us," she said as she walked ahead to answer the phone.

Suddenly she stopped dead in her tracks. "What? On my God. Trish, are you okay? Tell me where you are and we'll be there as soon as we can."

By now the group had gathered around Suzy. "It's Michael. He's been shot by that crazy woman. He's in critical condition. We need to get back to New York ASAP."

Jason went into action, and a little over an hour later he, Madge, Suzy, and Ken were on a private plane heading to Teterboro, right outside New York City.

33

LIFE AND DEATH

Part of Trish wished she was heading to Vermont with Suzy and Madge, but she didn't want to cancel the two workshops she had scheduled this weekend. Even though it was a holiday weekend, the two sessions were completely booked, one on Saturday afternoon and one on Sunday afternoon. Each was part of an eight-series workshop. This afternoon's was "A Holistic Approach to Pain Management".

And tomorrow was the last in the workshop series, "Caring for You Too". It was designed for people like Arlene, who had attended every session, who were caring for a seriously ill person. Each session featured experts in elder care, dealing with dementia and Alzheimer's, terminal illnesses, and making those difficult decisions, and most important, taking care of yourself.

She had just walked into the gallery to set up for the Saturday workshop when her cell phone rang. It was Michael. They'd been talking more and more lately on the phone, sometimes for as long as an hour. Michael would tell her about his students and how much he was enjoying teaching. She'd share the latest updates on The Three Tomatoes.

Neither of them mentioned the elephant in the room but it had been weeks since Lacey had done anything overt, and they cautiously started to feel comfortable that she was disappearing from their lives.

Trish answered her phone. "Hey, Trish, it's me. I was hoping to catch you before your workshop starts."

"I'm just setting up. What's going on?"

"Well, I have really exciting news I want to tell you about."

"Great, so tell me."

"Actually, I was hoping we could meet and I could tell you in person."

There was silence on Trish's end.

"Trish? Could we meet for a drink or dinner tonight?"

No, no, no, Trish thought. *I'm not ready for dinner with Michael. Who knows where that would lead?*

"Well, I can't do dinner. But what if we have an early lunch tomorrow? You could meet me at the gallery and we can head somewhere close by. I have a workshop that starts at 2:00 p.m."

"I'll be there by noon."

"Yep, see you then."

***

Trish was wide-awake at 6:00 a.m. Sunday morning. She was actually really excited about seeing Michael, and curious about his exciting news too. She went for a long run along the East River Greenway. She jogged past the 34th Street Heliport and with thoughts of Michael whirling in her head, went almost to Battery Park before she realized it. She got back in time to shower and to take some extra time with her hair and makeup. Yikes, she thought. You'd think this was a date. Well actually it felt like a date.

She got to the gallery at eleven to start setting up for her workshop, and to be there before Michael arrived. And a few minutes before noon, there he was. He looked great. He had lost a few pounds and looked rested too. He was wearing his usual preppy casual clothes — khakis, a pink striped buttoned-down shirt, a navy sweater, and loafers.

"Trish, you look beautiful," he said as he kissed her on the cheek. "And wow, look at what you've done with the gallery."

Trish showed him how they had made a little office area in the back, and showed him the brochures of some of the workshops they were doing. "And once a month we do a large event in the theater across the street. Next month's is already sold out. It's titled 'Does Sexy Have an Expiration Date?'"

"Well, looking at you, Trish, the answer to that is hell no!" laughed Michael. "So where should we go to lunch?"

Five minutes later they were seated outside at one the Village's many little cozy cafés. It was a beautiful day without a cloud in the sky. When she thought back on this day, she'd always remember how perfectly it had started out.

She ordered a healthy organic salad, and Michael ordered a rare burger with fries, and looked over to see Trish smiling at him. "Well, I know I should have ordered the salad too, but you know I've never met a burger I didn't love."

Trish laughed. It was good to feel like them again. "So, what's this exciting news of yours?"

"I thought you'd never ask," Michael chuckled. "Well, I have just been offered an Endowed Chair at Columbia's School of Business to create a new series of courses on Wall Street ethics. And I've accepted."

"Michael, that's wonderful news!"

Over lunch, Michael told her how much he was really enjoying teaching. "I love being back on campus and having thoughtful conversations with smart people. And the chance to mold some

216

young business minds and make them aware of the pitfalls of Wall Street, as well as the highs, is a legacy I'd like to leave. And while I certainly won't be making the kind of money I had been, it's a good salary with excellent benefits. It would give us a chance to start a new and simpler life together, Trish." Michael reached over and took her hand in his. "I love you, Trish, and I want you back in my life. Will you consider it?"

Trish looked into his eyes for a long time. "Yes, Michael, I'll consider it. But let's take it slow."

"Slow is better than no, so I'd say that's an optimistic sign."

They ate lunch, chatting about Michael's new opportunity, some of his favorite teaching moments, and the growing success of The Three Tomatoes. "Oh my gosh, I have to get back," Trish said, realizing the time had flown by.

Michael got the check and they strolled back to the gallery. Michael walked inside with her and said, "Trish, this was great today. I've missed you so, so much."

"And I've missed you," Trish said, as Michael embraced her, and their lips met in a passionate kiss.

Just as they were pulling away, the door to the gallery flung open. "You bitch! I told you he's mine." It was Lacey, with the most evil face Trish had ever seen, and she was brandishing a gun. "I'll kill you, cunt," she said aiming the gun at Trish. Just as she was about to pull the trigger, Michael threw himself in front of Trish and the gun went off.

As Michael was falling to the ground, Lacey pointed the gun back at Trish. Just then the door flung open again, and a giant of a man grabbed Lacey and pinned her to the floor, pulled out his cell phone, and called 911.

Trish was screaming. There was blood everywhere, and there was her Michael, her beautiful Michael, lying in a pool of it. She bent down to cradle his head in her lap. She barely remembered the police and ambulance arriving. "Where are you taking him?" she shouted.

"To Bellevue."

And then she felt a burly arm around her. It was the giant who had come through the door and grabbed Lacey and saved her. "Don't worry, I'll get you to Bellevue."

"Who are you?" Trish finally had the wherewithal to ask this stranger, on the way to the hospital.

"I'm a bodyguard. I was hired to follow Lacey and protect you and your husband from her. But she slipped away from me this morning. I'll never forgive myself."

"You were hired to protect us? Who hired you?" Trish asked incredulously.

"I'm afraid I can't divulge that information."

The second they arrived, Trish ran into the emergency room, frantic for information. "You'll have to wait here until the doctors have seen your husband," the perfunctory receptionist informed Trish. "Just have a seat."

In shock, Trish sat down. In a fog, she heard someone saying, "Mrs. Hogan, can we have a word with you?" She looked up at two police officers. "Can you tell us what happened?" Before she could say anything, the burly stranger appeared and told the cops he had been hired as a bodyguard and could fill them in on the details.

Trish looked down and realized she was covered in blood. She was shaking from head to toe when she felt a gentle hand on her arm. She looked up to see Arlene standing there.

"Oh, Trish, oh my God. I'm so sorry. I got to the gallery just as they were putting Michael into the ambulance. I got here as fast as I could." She sat down next to Trish and took her hand.

"Michael was shot trying to save me," Trish cried. "He was trying to save me."

"Mrs. Hogan?" A nurse was now standing in front of Trish and Arlene. "They're taking your husband into the OR. They won't know the extent of his injuries until they can get in and take a look, but right now he is critical. They'll do everything they can. You can head to the third floor OR waiting room and we'll keep you updated."

Trish looked like she was about to collapse. Arlene grabbed her arm, and led her into the ladies' room. "Here, Trish. Change into these. They're my yoga clothes. I was heading to a class after our workshop. Then wash your face, and we'll go upstairs and wait and pray."

***

When Suzy, Madge, Ken, and Jason arrived at the hospital three hours later, Michael was still in surgery. Arlene filled them in on the little they knew. "He was shot in the stomach and the damage is extensive."

Suzy and Madge sat on either side of Trish, just holding her hands.

An hour later the surgeon came out. "You husband is alive, but he is in critical condition. We had to remove his spleen and the bullet did a lot of damage to his internal organs. We've repaired what we can, but there's a great deal of bleeding and if he continues to hemorrhage we might not be able to stop it. The next twenty-four hours are critical. They're setting him up in ICU. But please no more than two people at a time. We need room for emergency care for him as needed."

For the next twenty-four hours, they rotated staying in the room with Trish and Michael. Trish refused to leave his side. He was still unconscious, but he was alive.

"He's still not out of the woods," the doctor explained the next afternoon. "But the bleeding seems to have stabilized and that's a good sign. Mrs. Hogan, I think you should try to get a little sleep, and come back later."

Trish refused to leave. Madge went back to the apartment and grabbed some clean clothes and a toothbrush for Trish, plus the little velvet box on the dresser that Trish asked her to bring back to the hospital.

By the third day, Michael was still in a coma. They were all gathered outside Michael's room for an update. "Listen, I'm not going to sugarcoat this," the doctor said. "The severe loss of blood may have caused brain damage, and the longer he stays in a coma, the more that seems possible. At this point, there is nothing medically we can do."

Trish had sat by Michael's bedside, just praying for a miracle. At ten o'clock that night, she got it. She looked up and saw Michael's eyelids fluttering. And then they fluttered a little more, and then he opened his eyes. "Quick, get a nurse," she shouted to Suzy who had dozed off in the chair next to her.

Trish and Suzy were told to wait outside. Fifteen minutes later, the doctor came out and said, "Well, I have good news. Your husband is awake and alert. He's got a lot of healing to do, but I think he's going to make it. You can see him for a few minutes, but please do not tire him out."

Trish collapsed into Suzy's arms. After she returned to Michael's room and he whispered, "I love you," before going back to sleep, which the doctor assured her was normal, she left the hospital for the first time in four days. She went back to Madge's apartment and slept for eight solid hours.

The next day they moved Michael to a regular room and downgraded his condition from critical to serious.

Trish sat by his bedside, holding his hand. Michael wanted to know everything that had happened. The last thing he remembered was kissing Trish in the gallery. Trish filled him in on the rest. "Michael, you got shot trying to save me from Lacey. And after she shot you, she was about to shoot me too when this bodyguard appeared from nowhere and took her down."

"A bodyguard? Am I that confused that I don't know about this?"

"No, sweetheart. I didn't know either. Jason fessed up that when we said no to his offer to hire bodyguards to protect us, he hired one to follow Lacey around. If he hadn't done that, we might both be dead right now."

"And where's Lacey?"

"She's locked away in a prison psych ward, where hopefully she will stay for a long, long time."

"Oh, Trish, I am so sorry. This is all my fault. I don't know how I could have been so stupid to get involved with her. And if something had happened to you I could never have forgiven myself."

"Michael, stop. It's over. And I have something for you."

"What?"

"Open your hand." And with that, Trish took the other key that Michael had given her on Christmas Eve, and put it into the palm of his hand. "Here's the key to my heart, which you will have forever."

34

ON THE MEND

Two weeks later, Michael was released from the hospital. Jason and Madge had convinced them to go to the farm in Vermont for Michael to recuperate.

"Trish, the timing is perfect," said Madge. "You were going to put the workshops and monthly events on hold until the fall anyway. And Michael doesn't return to school until the end of August. This will give Michael the summer to recover and both of you a chance to rediscover each other. And you know how calm and peaceful it is there. Plus, you'll have us there for part of the time, for fun and company."

Michael and Trish agreed, and Jason insisted that they fly there in a private plane at his expense.

The next afternoon, the four of them were sitting on the front veranda of Jason's farm, sipping ice teas and enjoying the mountain views. They had an early dinner, and after Trish got Michael settled into bed and asleep, she came back downstairs and joined Madge and Jason at the fire pit. Madge had a glass of wine waiting for her.

"I don't know how to even begin to thank you. This is just what we needed. There's no way we could have gone back to Michael's apartment. This gives us time to sort things out and figure out where we'll live this fall too. So now, enough about Michael and me. What's happening in your lives?"

"Well now that I've sold Snazzed, I really want to focus on my foundation and how we can make a real impact. And as Madge said to me, I can't see the world from behind a desk or sitting on a tractor at the farm. So, one of the things Madge and I have talked about is going on some humanitarian missions to parts of the world that are in desperate need. That way I can see firsthand where the needs are, meet some of the organizations that are on the ground, and discover how we can help."

"And we've come up with an idea that can fit under The Three Tomatoes umbrella," added Madge. "Suzy's excited about it and I want to share it with you too."

"Pour me some more wine and I'm all ears," said Trish.

"Well, right now in East Africa, there is a hunger crisis of unprecedented levels. Literally millions of people will starve to death without help. And the mainstream media barely covers this. So, I've called some UN friends of mine and Jason and I are joining a fact-finding mission there. And here's where The Three Tomatoes comes in. I'm bringing a film crew and we'll start publicizing this crisis through The Three Tomatoes and any other outlets that will cover it. It's appalling what's happening," said Madge. "These are the kinds of stories I wanted to tell when I was at the network, but they always gave short shrift to it."

"Madge, I had no idea that kind of crisis was even happening. When do you and Jason leave?"

"In about three weeks. We'll be there for about two weeks on the ground."

"I think that's terrific. And, Jason, before the craziness, I had started to think about ideas on how your foundation can support women's health initiatives too, if that's something you're still interested in."

"Absolutely. What are you thinking?"

"Well, our traditional medical approach is siloed. It's as if each part of our body functions separately from the rest of us. That's why we have a specialty for everything. But the more enlightened medical professionals understand that the body, and mind too, are integrated, and we need to approach our health from an integrated standpoint that includes traditional and nontraditional health treatments. Not to mention that we have very few facilities that focus only on women's health," Trish explained.

"And what would you do about that? "asked Jason.

"I'd love to see a truly integrated women's health center in New York City, that's available to all women, regardless of whether their insurance covers it or not. It could be a model for other cities around the country."

"I like your thinking, Trish. And I experienced a lot of what you're saying when Abigail was diagnosed with cancer the second time. Could you put together a list of some of the top integrated health people you're familiar with? I'd like to get them all in a room and explore how we could make your vision happen."

"I'd love to do that, and it's something I can do this summer while Michael is recovering."

"So, Madge, is Suzy okay with running the day-to-day operations of The Three Tomatoes over the summer? I'm feeling a little guilty that she may feel we've deserted her. And let's not forget she has a grandchild on the way too."

"I was concerned too," said Madge. "I was going to postpone the trip to Africa, but Suzy insists that all is in control. Having staff now helps enormously, and the Arpello launch is in the hands of Margot's marketing team and their new agency, so the summer's looking like clear sailing."

"And by the way, there's a Ripe Tomatoes dinner in two weeks. Bertha can stay with Michael, and Chrissy's here, so he'll be in good hands. So, if you can come back to New York for a few days we can have a status meeting with Suzy too."

"Well, if Michael keeps up his excellent progress, I will definitely do that. It could be a good chance for me to start looking for places for us to live too."

Trish took another sip of wine and looked up in the beautiful Vermont night sky.

"You know, right now I feel like the luckiest girl in the world. And one thing's for sure, I have the best friends in the world."

35

BORN AND REBORN

It was the last week in June, and the farm was working its magic on Michael and Trish too. With Bertha's homecooked healthy meals, he was putting on weight, and Trish made sure they went walking every day.

"Michael, are you sure you'll be okay for a few days while I'm back in New York?" said Trish.

"Of course. I'm getting stronger every day and Bertha won't let me get away with anything," he said as he winked at Bertha.

"Don't worry, Mrs. Hogan. I'll keep a close eye on him. He needs some more fattening up and I'll make sure he's out walking everyday too."

"Okay. And Bertha be sure to call me if he's not behaving." She heard the car horn beeping. "Well, I've got to run. Chrissy's driving me to the airport.

When she landed in New York after the short flight, she grabbed a cab at LaGuardia and had him wait while she dropped her bags at Madge's apartment building and then headed straight to their offices at the loft to meet Suzy and Madge. She definitely wasn't ready to go back to the gallery yet, even though she knew everything had been cleaned up and Suzy and Madge assured her there were no physical signs of the carnage there. But in Trish's head, it would always be there.

When Trish walked in, the growing Three Tomatoes staff all ran to her. They hugged, they cried, and then she and Suzy and Madge got down to their status meeting.

Suzy reported that their subscriber base had grown considerably once they started advertising. Their social media maven was doing a great job too, and the traffic to their website was now ten times what it had been two months ago.

Suzy also walked them through the exciting plans they had to launch the Arpello campaign at The Three Tomatoes. "We'll start with social media teasers, and then launch the first video spot on our home page. It will be exclusive to our site for the first three days." Suzy was convinced that once the Arpello campaign launched successfully, then other advertisers would follow.

"So, everything is going well," Suzy continued. "And with summer here, things will slow down a bit. Madge, it's a perfect time for you and Jason to head to Africa, and for Trish and Michael to recover too."

"It's so great to be back here with the two of you," said Trish. "What would I ever do without your love and support? And I'm really looking forward to our Ripe Tomatoes dinner tonight. Where shall we have our predinner martinis?"

***

When the three of then arrived for dinner and approached their usual table, all of the Ripe Tomatoes and the restaurant staff stood and applauded Trish as she walked in. Trish even saw a little tear come down the cheek of their longtime curmudgeon waiter.

They settled in and their waiter poured champagne, compliments of the restaurant.

Hope raised her glass. "Here's to our precious Trish. We are so happy to have you here with us tonight and we wish Michael a speedy recovery and much happiness to you both forever."

Suzy had asked Hope not to talk about the actual incident, but to focus on Trish's future.

"So, Trish, what's next for you and Michael?" Hope asked.

Trish told them that Michael was making a remarkable recovery and was looking forward to his new role at Columbia. "Now, I just have to find a place for us to live," she added.

"I might be able to help with that," said Angela, one of their Ripe Tomatoes who just happened to be owner of one of the city's top real estate firms. "You know Harlem's really the hot spot these days, and it's an easy commute for Michael to Columbia. And the subways are all there, so you could get downtown easily too. I could show you some lovely renovated brownstones that are reasonably priced, compared to the rest of the city." She and Trish made a date to meet the very next morning.

They continued sharing updates around the table. Madge filled them in on her upcoming trip to Africa. They were all shocked that they knew so little about the hunger crisis.

And when they got to Arlene, she gave them the not unexpected news that she had finally put Harry into a facility that specializes in caring for Alzheimer's patients. "It was a very difficult decision, but it was really Trish's workshops that got me through it. And I've already told Trish that I'd like to be part of the next workshops to help others."

They finally got back to Hope. Suzy could tell she was about to burst with her news, which she had shared in confidence with Suzy the day before.

"Well, ladies, Celeste and I have big, big news." She paused for dramatic effect. "We're heading to Broadway. *If Tomorrow Never Comes* will open in October."

They were all thrilled. "Oh and by the way, not to be catty, but Ellen's show is closing in two weeks. When she didn't get any of the off-Broadway awards this season, ticket sales went into the toilet."

They continued catching up and there was much joy and laughter around the table. Suzy realized her phone was buzzing in her purse. She had turned off the ringer. She quickly looked and saw she had several texts from Ken.

She leaped up from table. "I have to leave right now. Ian's baby is on the way. I'm about to become a grandmother."

"Well, we're going with you," said Trish and Madge simultaneously, and the three of them were out the door.

They grabbed a cab and told him to step on it to get them to New York-Presbyterian Lawrence Hospital in Bronxville. Suzy was on the phone with Ken. "But it's too early for her to be having the baby."

Ken explained they were trying to delay the birth but then her water broke. "Emily's in labor right now."

When they arrived on the maternity floor, they were greeted by Ken, who was beaming. "Well, you're officially a grandma. It's a girl. She only weighs four pounds and she's in NICU but the doctors have assured us she'll be fine. She'll need to stay in the hospital for a couple of weeks."

"Oh my gosh, when can we see her?"

"Well, we can go right now. Don't be upset, she's on oxygen to help her little lungs, and IVs, but she's just beautiful."

When they got to NICU, there was Ian inside standing next to an incubator gazing with wonderment at his tiny little daughter. He looked up and waved to them. Suzy thought her heart would explode with love.

***

Three days later, Trish was having dinner with Madge and Jason. They had all gone to see the baby again. Suzy was thrilled because they had let her into the NICU and she was allowed to hold her granddaughter for the first time.

"I've never seen a baby so tiny, and so perfect," said Jason. "And the look of such pure love on Suzy's face was priceless."

Madge felt a little stab in her heart. *Jason would make a great dad,* she thought. *And I'll never be able to give that to him.*

She wanted to change the subject and quickly turned to Trish and asked how the apartment search was going.

"I don't want to get too excited, but I think I might have found the perfect place for us. Angela is right. Harlem has undergone a major renaissance and she took me to see this one brownstone that's just about to come on the market. I have to do some number crunching with Michael, but I think with his new salary, and mine that we can swing it. It has so much charm and history. Beautiful high ceilings, working fireplaces, and a lovely little outdoor patio. And Michael could walk to work."

"Well, you know if you need help with the financing," Jason started to say before Trish cut him off.

"Jason, we appreciate everything you have done for us. But I can't accept another thing. And I think we'll be fine."

***

Jason joined Madge out on the terrace of the loft when they returned home from dinner, with two glasses of brandy.

"Honey, you're looking very pensive," he said to Madge. "Is something wrong?"

Madge turned to him, with tears in her eyes. "I saw the look on your face tonight when you were watching Suzy with the baby. You'd be a great father, Jason. And if you stay with me you'll never get that chance."

Jason took her in his arms. "Madge, I've told you so many times. You are all I need. We'll have a wonderful life together. And hopefully through the foundation we can help a lot of children around the world. That's more than enough for me."

***

The next morning Michael and Trish went through all the numbers on the phone. She had sent him photos of the brownstone and then described it in detail. Michael agreed it sounded perfect.

"Trish, it will be a squeeze, but we can do it."

"But, Michael, I'd be making this commitment without your even seeing the place."

"Sweetheart, I trust you 100 percent. The pictures and your description are all I need. And honestly, I'd be happy in a studio apartment with you. But you know if we don't grab this now, it will be gone. It's a great deal."

"Okay," said Trish, "I'll make the offer today."

Later that afternoon she called Michael. "Harlem, here we come!"

***

Ken walked into the bedroom with a steaming cup of coffee for Suzy, who was just rousing. He put it on her nightstand, and leaned over and kissed her. "You know, you are just about the sexiest grandma on the planet."

"And you're not bad for being a grandpa, yourself." Ken sat on the side on the bed while Suzy sipped her coffee.

"I'm so proud of our son," Suzy continued. "It's still tough for me to wrap my brain around the idea that our baby has a baby, but when I look at him now, over the past two weeks, I see a man."

"I see it too," said Ken. "It's not going to be easy for them, and, heck, who knows if he and Emily will even stay together, but I do know that Ian will always do the right thing. And he'll be there for his daughter. I guess we did okay raising him," Ken said. His hands were now under the covers, and had moved their way up to Suzy's breasts.

"You know, I've never made love to a grandma before," he said, as he climbed back into bed.

"Well, dear," Suzy whispered in his ear after their lovemaking, "I'd say that was quite an impressive performance...especially for a grandpa."

36

AWAKENING

Jason and Madge were on their way to a third refugee camp in as many days. This one was in Ethiopia. The story had been the same everywhere — from the South Sudan, to Nigeria, to here — millions of people were starving, many of them children.

With Madge's film crew rolling their cameras, their UN guide told them that half a million children in northeastern Nigeria are so severely malnourished that seventy-five thousand could die in the next month. A growing measles outbreak in the region could transform into an epidemic too. And malaria outbreaks were yet another crisis.

"The drought here in Ethiopia," he continued, "is the worst in fifty years. Eighteen million people are in dire need. Mothers are walking many miles a day and more just to bring water back to their children."

Jason was shocked by what he had seen and heard. But he was also learning that it was much more complicated than just throwing money at the problem and hoping that would fix things. Widespread corruption, a lack of infrastructure, and a lack of leadership were parts of the problem. Jason was looking for the pockets of hope with groups and community leaders on the ground who knew what it would take to make a difference.

"You were so right," Jason said to Madge from his cot in their tent that night. "I could never have gotten an understanding of what's happening here, sitting behind a desk. How do we even begin to help?"

"I know. It can get overwhelming," Madge said reaching out to Jason's cot to hold his hand. "That's when I'm reminded of something Mother Teresa said, 'I alone cannot change the world, but I can cast a stone across the waters to create many ripples.' I'm hoping with the images we've captured on film this week that we might be able to create a few ripples."

"That's a good thought to go to sleep with," Jason said. "And we have another big day tomorrow at one of the orphanages."

The next morning, they were escorted to an orphanage compound about twenty miles away. There were several low buildings, surrounded by barbed wire fencing. There was a small dirt courtyard in the center, where children were running around. Their guide today was from UNICEF.

"The orphans here are lucky. They actually have a roof over their heads, and food to eat. But sadly, in Ethiopia alone there are 4.5 million orphans. Their parents have either died of AIDS, untreated illnesses, hunger, drought, or war. Many of these children are fending for themselves. Come inside, and we'll meet the director."

Just as Madge was about to walk through the door, she was hit in the back by a soccer ball. She turned around to see a little boy, who looked around five, wide-eyed and frightened that he had hurt her.

"It's okay, it's okay," she said gently and tossed the ball back his way.

The orphanage director gave them a tour, apologizing along the way. "We do the best we can with limited resources. We try to give each child their own bed, but sometimes that is not possible," he explained as they walked through the dormitory rooms jam-packed with cots and bunk beds. And then there were the babies, sometimes two in a crib. Many of them were crying.

"We try to comfort them when we can, but we just do not have enough staff to provide much more than the necessities."

They were back out in the hallway now, when Madge spied the little boy with the soccer ball peering around the corner at them. She gave him a little wave and he disappeared.

Madge had secured permission to do some filming at the orphanage. Jason was invited into the director's office to talk in more detail about the orphan crisis and what could be done.

She had brought some books and toys for the children, and as soon as she opened the bag she felt like the Pied Piper. Children were following her everywhere. Out of the corner of her eye, she kept seeing the little soccer boy watching her intently, although he didn't approach her.

It was soon time for lunch, and the children were all called into a large room with long tables. They were served a hearty soup, and each child had a carton of milk. The aid explained that was a treat. "We just got a delivery from UNICEF. Most often we're watering down fruit juices for the children."

Madge was talking with one of her video guys to see what he had captured on film, when she felt a tug on her pants. She looked down and there was her little friend. He was pointing to the camera.

"Oh, do you want to see?" Madge said. And then realizing he did not understand English, she brought the camera down to his level, and showed him the footage they had just taken. She could tell he was fascinated.

She showed him how to push some of the buttons. And then handed him the camera and gestured for him to take a video of her.

He shyly took the camera, and Madge made funny faces while he filmed her with the help of the cameraman.

She then played back the video and that was when he broke out in a smile that could bring the sun out.

"Yonas, Yonas," the aid spoke to him in Amharic, shooing him away.

"Oh, it's fine," said Madge. "He's not bothering us. He can follow us around." Which he did for the rest of the afternoon.

"Who's your little friend?" Jason asked, when he emerged from his meeting with the director and a small group from UNICEF.

"This is Yonas. Yonas, this is Jason."

Jason put his hand out to shake Yonas's but the little boy scurried behind Madge. "I think he has to get to know you first."

The director invited them to stay for dinner in the staff dining room. "We're serving soup tonight. And after dinner, if you like, you can help to put the children to sleep. They love a comforting hand and we don't have enough of those around here."

After dinner, Jason and Madge went into one of the large dormitories. They each had a copy of *Goodnight Moon* that Madge had brought along. They each sat on a bed and were immediately surrounded by children. As Madge started to read, pointing out the photos, Yonas made his way closer to her and soon was sitting on her lap. Jason glanced over, and thought that was the most beautiful sight he had ever seen.

Long after they had returned to their campsite and into their cots, Madge was still wide-awake. Then she thought she heard Jason rouse. "Jason, are you awake?"

"Hmm, sort of," he said groggily.

"Oh sorry, go back to sleep."

"No, no I'm awake, now. What's keeping you awake?"

"I can't stop thinking about Yonas. He's such a special little boy. I wonder what his story is?"

"We can find out when we go back tomorrow. The director has the backgrounds on most of the children, or at least the ones who are up for adoption. Not all of them are though... Only the ones who they know for sure have parents that died."

They returned the next day. There were children playing in the courtyard, but Madge was disappointed that Yonas wasn't one of them. They had moved into the director's office with the camera crew. He had agreed to let Madge interview him. Madge had just sat down next to the director to start when she noticed a little brown head peeking around the corner. It was Yonas.

"So, what is the process for adopting children here?" Madge asked.

"Well, first we have to be able to certify that both of the child's parents are dead. Unfortunately, in many cases, that is not possible, and those children can never be officially adopted. There is of course an application process, and a vetting process. But often we can cut through the red tape, and place a child in his or her new home quickly."

"Can a single person adopt a child?"

"Yes, but that process can take much longer. Our government prefers that married couples adopt."

When the interview was finished, Madge realized that Yonas had left. *I guess he got bored,* she thought.

"Please stay for lunch," the director said. "Today we have leftover soup."

As the crew was removing the equipment, Madge went to find Jason. There he was in the courtyard, showing a group of boys that included Yonas, how to strike the soccer ball. When Yonas looked up and saw Madge, he left the group and ran toward her and gave her a huge hug.

Over lunch with the director, Madge said, "So, tell me a little about Yonas." And trying to act casual, asked, "Is he up for adoption?"

"Ah, Yonas. He's one of our favorites around here. He turns five next month. And he's incredibly smart. He's been with us since he was three years old. He spent several months in a hospital first. He arrived here severely malnourished and weighed only twenty pounds. It's amazing that it didn't affect his mental capacities. His father was killed in the war. His mother was brutally raped and died of AIDS. Sadly, this is not a unique story."

Madge sucked in a deep breath. "That is a sad story. I hope he finds a loving home."

Jason sat in silence.

Just as they were getting ready to leave, Yonas ran to Madge before she could reach the Jeep. He had *Goodnight Moon* in his hands and tugged at her to stay. She took his little hand in hers, walked back inside, and sat down and read the book to him. She then quickly walked to the Jeep, keeping her head down so no one would see the tears running down her cheeks.

That night, once again, Madge couldn't sleep. She thought she heard Jason stirring again.

"Sweetheart," she whispered.

"Yes!" he answered emphatically.

"Yes, what? I haven't asked you anything yet."

"Yes. We have to adopt Yonas."

37

WEDDING BELLS

It was a hot and humid day at the end of July. Suzy had just ordered a martini and was saving two seats at the bar at Balthazar when Trish and Madge walked in.

"It's so fucking hot, my panties are melting," said Madge.

Suzy started to laugh. "I think you said that same thing the last time we were here — and that was almost a year ago."

When Trish's and Madge's martinis arrived, and glasses were clinked, Suzy said, "Well, it's great to be together again. We have so much to catch up on."

Suzy proudly shared photos of her granddaughter, Elsa. "She's been home for a week and Ian is staying at Emily's parents' home with them. Her parents have been great, and they don't seem to mind my daily visits at all. She is just so precious, I tear up every time I hold her."

"Elsa is a lovely name," said Trish. "Is that a family name?"

"Well, only if you're a Disney. Seems Emily has watched *Frozen* dozens of times." They all laughed.

"So, what's their plan?" asked Trish.

"Emily rejected Ian's marriage proposal, which frankly both sets of parents breathed a sigh of relief over. And Emily has convinced Ian that he has to go back to Princeton when school starts. She's going to take online courses this semester so she can be with the baby. And Ian's close enough that he can come home when he wants. So, we'll see how it goes."

Trish told them Michael's doctors were very pleased with his recovery and saw no reason why he shouldn't return to teaching when the semester starts.

"Michael came back from Vermont with me, and we're closing on the brownstone tomorrow. We'll stay in the city at Madge's for now so we can get everything set to move into our new home before the end of August. I feel like a newlywed. And, Madge, we want to hear all about your trip to Africa. You must be exhausted since you just got back yesterday."

"Actually, I'm too excited to feel exhausted. But sticking with this theme of babies and proposals and newlyweds, I have big news."

Madge told them all about the trip and the suffering of millions of people. "The situation is more desperate than you can imagine, and the need for stepped-up humanitarian help is critical."

She told them the story of the orphanage and meeting Yonas. "The orphanage is a heartbreaking place. But these children are the fortunate ones, since many children are on their own and begging on the streets. All of the children in the orphanage touch your heart, but it was love at first sight with Yonas. Something inside me just opened up the moment I looked into his beautiful big brown eyes.

"And Jason felt the same way. We stayed up all night when we made the decision to adopt Yonas. And when Jason dropped down on one knee of the floor of our tent, and asked me to marry him, I said yes without any hesitation. When Jason stood up and dusted the dirt off his knee, we burst out laughing.

"And then Jason told me before we left for Africa, he'd planned a very romantic scenario to propose to me when we returned home.

"And it definitely wasn't on one knee on a dusty tent floor in the middle of a desert. He told me the ring was in his bureau dresser in the loft, just waiting to be put on my finger."

With that, Madge held out her left hand, which she had surreptitiously been hiding. There on her finger was a modest, but beautiful, antique diamond ring. "It was Jason's grandmother's."

Suzy and Trish were starting to well up with tears. "Tell us everything about Yonas."

"Well," continued Madge, "the next morning, we returned to the orphanage and told the director we wanted to adopt him. He was as excited as we were. And when we told him we were heading back to the States to get married, he said that would make the process much easier. Then he called in Yonas and asked him if he would like us to be his new parents and live in America. Yonas leaped in my lap and put his little arms around my neck and hugged me until his arms got tired." She then showed them pictures they took of Yonas before they left.

Suzy and Trish were overcome with emotion for their friend.

"Wow, I don't even know where to begin to process all this," said Suzy. "This will take another martini. And I have a zillion questions."

As the second martinis arrived, Trish asked, "So when are you getting married and how long will it take to get Yonas here?"

"It's really short notice, but we'd like to get married on the farm over Labor Day weekend. And this might sound silly at our ages, but would you be my bridesmaids? And I promise I won't make you wear those hideous frilly gowns I had to wear at each of your weddings."

Suzy and Madge jumped with joy! "We're going to be bridesmaids, and aunties too."

"And in terms of getting Yonas here, I don't mind saying I'm pulling every favor I can call in from diplomats and politicians to get him here quickly — if we're lucky, by Christmas. My only regret is that we can't take every one of those precious children. But we have some excellent footage from the trip, and hopefully that will open up other opportunities for these kids and more support for the orphanages too."

"Oh my God, wait until you tell the Ripe Tomatoes tonight. I can't wait to see the looks on their faces," said Suzy. "Let's head over there."

***

Even though she was bursting, Madge waited until the end of dinner to share her news. "And I want you all at the wedding."

They were so excited and all talking at once that their waiter rushed over thinking something was wrong.

"Quite the opposite," explained Hope. "Nothing could be righter."

Suzy called Ken and asked him to wait up because she had "exciting news". Ken greeted her at the door. "So, what's up?"

"Well, this news requires a glass of champagne, and deserves more than a foyer announcement."

They moved into the kitchen where Ken popped some bubbly while Suzy gave him the news.

"Well, I'll be damned," said Ken with a huge grin on his face.

"I know. Last year at this time, I was working at that 'horrid little agency', as Margot would say. Madge was miserable at the network and her idea of romance was a half-night stand. Trish's world was about to crumble, and becoming grandparents was something that was way off in the future. It's been quite the year."

"I'll drink to that," said Ken as they clinked glasses.

38

JUST DUES

Madge and Suzy were working in the conference room at the loft. Trish was at her new brownstone supervising the painters.

"I wish we could get Trish back into the gallery. I know she keeps postponing the start dates of the fall workshops because she's still traumatized," said Suzy.

Madge agreed. "Well, it will take time. And who knows, she might never want to go back there. We might have to think about another space for the workshops."

Madge went back to her computer where she had been viewing some of their Africa footage. "Suzy, come take a look at some of these edited clips. I think I should start posting these five-minute clips and I'll write blog posts around them. We could do a series."

Suzy sat and watched. When the last clip finished, she sat there in silence.

"Suzy? What do you think?"

When Suzy turned around to face Madge there were tears streaming down her cheeks. "Madge, that is one of the most moving pieces of journalism I have seen in a long time. I think you should turn this into a documentary."

"Well, I've been thinking about that. I want to get this story out to as many people as possible. But in the meantime, I'll post the first clip at our web site and on our YouTube channel. August is a slow news month so maybe it will get some attention."

By the end of the week, the first video clip had over one million views. The following week Madge posted a second clip with her blog and that one got over five million views.

Trish, Suzy, and Madge were all in the conference room high-fiving when Madge's cell rang. Madge walked to a corner of the room to take the call.

Trish was telling Suzy that she and Michael were moving into the brownstone over the coming weekend, when Madge let out a "Holy shit, hell has frozen over" scream.

"What is going on?" asked Suzy.

"That was the producer of *Good Morning New York*. They want me to come on the show Friday to talk with 'big tits in the camera'

Heather about the famine crisis. I said yes, so I guess that cold day in hell is here."

Trish and Suzy were ecstatic. "Oh, Madge, that's great. You'll be getting this story out there to even more people," said Trish.

"And not to sound too self-promoting, you'll be getting The Three Tomatoes name out there too," added Suzy.

***

Madge arrived at the studio before the start of the show even though she was scheduled for the last segment of the morning. She wanted to see some of the old gang. She hesitated for a second before walking into the studio. She was feeling a little unnerved. After all, it had been a year now since she quit, and she knew some of the show staffers felt she had left them high and dry. "Oh well, just suck it up," she thought as she pushed through the double-glass doors.

She was immediately greeted with cheers of "Welcome back, Madge," and the entire crew standing in applause. She made her way around the group giving hugs and kisses, and then heard that distinctive purring voice, "Madge, so good to have you back."

She turned around to face Heather Big Tits. "I'm really impressed with the work you're doing, and I know this will be a great segment today," said Heather and then turned and headed to the makeup room.

Hmmm...that almost seemed sincere, thought Madge.

She hung out with the crew until it was time for her segment. It was the usual five minutes covering the highlights, but Heather actually took a back seat and let Madge tell the the story.

When the cameras stopped rolling, Madge thanked Heather for the opportunity.

"Well, as I said, you're doing impressive work," Heather replied.

Madge was about to leave the set when Heather surprised her with, "Do you have time for a cup of coffee? There's something I want to talk to you about."

"Ahhh...well sure," Madge replied.

"Just give me a few minutes to get some of this makeup off and I'll meet you at the Starbucks downstairs."

This is odd, thought Madge as she found two seats in a quiet corner at Starbucks. *And why aren't we meeting in the executive dining room that's reserved for the execs and the on-air talent?*

As soon as they got their cappuccinos, Heather got right to the point.

"Listen, Madge, I know I'm not your favorite person. But I have something to tell you in confidence, and I'm hoping you might be able to help."

"I'm all ears," said Madge, intrigued now.

"I'm filing a sexual harassment suit against Jack Feldy tomorrow. I know this will be the end of my career at the network, but I can't let this go on one day longer."

Madge was suddenly feeling light-headed. "Well, what, ah, what happened?"

"It's been going on since I started at the network three years ago. And I'm not proud to say I let it continue this long. At first, it was ass grabs when he'd pass by me. Then it was little tête-à-têtes in his office with a glass of bourbon. And yes, I know I should have walked out, but he was always telling me how he could make me the biggest star on the news network. So, I put up with his disgusting comments like, 'Baby, I'm hungry, and those big tits of yours look delicious.' And once when I'd had a little too much bourbon I actually let him suck one. When I left his office, I threw up.

"But last week was the final straw. His assistant called and asked if I could meet with Jack in his office around 8:00 p.m. I sort of hesitated, because as you know when you have to get up at the crack of dawn for a morning show, that's late. But she added that in strict confidence, she thought Jack had some exciting plans for me for the *That's All, Folks,* Sunday magazine show. There have been rumors that they were going to replace the current host.

"I was so excited. I got there a little before eight, and Jack's assistant said I could go into his office in a few minutes, that Jack was just finishing up a call. And would I excuse her because she was leaving for the day. So, I waited a couple of minutes, and then I knocked on Jack's door. He bellowed for me to come in. 'Close the door', he said, which I did. And when I turned around, he came from around his desk with no pants on. Nothing, stark naked with a huge hard-on. He must have taken Viagra. He strolled in front of the desk, like all was perfectly normal and told me to sit down. I was so scared, I did as he told me.

"'So, Heather, I've got some big things in store for you,' he said. He was now standing in front of me with that ugly cock in my face. 'We're considering you to be the next host of *That's All, Folks*. What do you think of that my little superstar?'

"I stammered, and kept pushing my chair back. Then he said, 'So now I think it's time you and I did a little celebrating,' and he tried to thrust himself into my mouth. I bit him. He screamed and called me a 'fucking cunt' and I ran out of the office.

"The next morning when I arrived at the studio, my dressing room was filled with flowers, and a note that said, 'Just a little misunderstanding.' And no signature."

Madge was pale now. "Heather, that's just horrible. I am so sorry. And it's very brave of you to stand up to him. You know how powerful he is."

"Well, this is where the favor comes in. As my lawyer said, this can't be the first time he's ever done this. And it would really help my case if I'm not the only one with these 'quote, unquote' allegations. So, my question is did he ever do anything to you or anyone else you know?"

There was a long pause before Madge responded. "Heather, I'm really sorry about what happened to you. I believe you, but I can't help." And with that she got up and hurried out of Starbucks.

39

THE RIGHT THING

My first commute from our new home, Trish thought as she boarded the Downtown 1 train in Harlem to the loft. It had been quite a busy weekend. They had moved in on Saturday and while there were still tons of boxes to unpack, she and Michael had never been happier. After the moving trucks left, they ordered pizza, brought a couple of kitchen chairs out into their little backyard, and opened a bottle of wine that they poured into paper cups.

Michael raised his cup and said, "To life, love, and new beginnings."

And then on Sunday they went to Bronxville for baby Elsa's christening.

"She's a miracle," Trish said to Suzy. "And Ian and Emily and the baby are a beautiful little family."

Suzy looked at them lovingly, and then sighed, "Yes, they are. I hope they stay that way."

It was a lovely party, but Trish couldn't help noticing how quiet Madge was all afternoon. She chalked it up to wedding jitters and the stress about getting the adoption finalized.

Her thoughts then turned to the fall workshops. She hadn't announced a schedule yet, and as Madge and Suzy had surmised, she couldn't even think about walking through the doors of the gallery. But she also hated the thought of incurring additional expenses to rent space for the workshops when the gallery was sitting there unused.

By the time she arrived at the loft, she had an idea, and knew she had to add this to today's status meeting.

Madge was already in the conference room when she arrived, followed about ten minutes later by Suzy who burst in shouting, "Did you read the front page of the *New York Post* this morning?"

"Yes," said Madge, displaying no emotions.

"What are two talking about?" asked Trish.

"Heather Stone is suing Jack Feldy for sexual harassment. And social media is all over it with appalling comments like, 'Well what do you expect when you wear low-cut dresses on air and flaunt your boobs everywhere?"

"God, that's awful," said Trish. "Talk about blaming the victim."

"He is just a disgusting pig. And of course, he's denying these 'unfounded' allegations," Suzy continued. And when she realized Madge had turned away, she stopped. "Madge, are you okay? You're unusually quiet on this bombshell."

"Listen, you know I don't like Heather, and she definitely flaunts her sexuality, but no one deserves to be sexually harassed by a man in power. No one," said Madge emphatically. "Now can we change the subject and start our status meeting?"

Whoa, thought Suzy. *Something's not right here. Maybe it's wedding jitters. It's only two weeks away.*

"Well, at least we don't have to worry about that at The Three Tomatoes," said Trish. "I'd like to add the workshops to today's status agenda."

They went over Madge's schedule first. The day after the wedding they were leaving for Ethiopia to see Yonas and do some more filming. Madge was now determined to turn this into a documentary.

"But we'll only be gone a week," she said.

"Madge, really, you and Jason should take a little time for a honeymoon while you're away," said Suzy. "Trish is back now, and we've got things in control."

"Oh, I know you do," said Madge. "But Jason and I want to stay on top of the adoption and there are things we have to do here too to make that happen. And I want to get back and start turning our footage into a documentary."

They next turned their attention to Trish.

"I want to restart the workshops in September, but I just can't go back to the gallery yet," Trish said. "I know we still have a paid-up lease through the end of the year, and I don't want us to incur more expenses by having to rent elsewhere. But I think I have an idea that might work."

One of Trish's many friends in the health and wellness arena had recently launched an integrated health center in Midtown. It was a three-story town house, and Trish's thought was to see if her friend would make one floor available for the workshops and in exchange, The Three Tomatoes would promote the Health Center. Madge and Suzy thought it was a great idea.

Trish reached out to her friend and by noon, reported, "Great news! We're all set, and we can start our next workshops by the middle of September."

***

On Friday morning Madge dragged herself out of bed. She hadn't fallen asleep until 5:00 a.m., and now just three hours later, her alarm was buzzing.

Jason had left the day before for the farm. Much to Madge's relief, Jason, Chrissy, and Bertha had gone into full-on wedding mode, and were making all the arrangements. If it had been up to Madge, she and Jason would have gotten married at City Hall. But Jason really wanted the wedding at the farm with their family and close friends there. He told Madge not to worry, they'd handle the details and he'd keep her in the loop.

It wasn't the wedding that was keeping her awake. It was fucking Jack Feldy. The full-out onslaught of his team of high-powered lawyers to smear Heather's reputation had escalated. The media and gossip rags were having a field day. It had been front page news every day this week.

This cannot go on, thought Madge. *And I'm the only one who can stop it.*

She texted Trish and Suzy, and told them when they arrived to head up to the living quarters at the loft. She had something personal she wanted to discuss with them.

Suzy was on her way into the city when she got the text. Her first thought was that Madge was getting cold feet about the wedding. *Well, Trish and I will just give her a little pep talk and get her down off the cliff. Jason is the best thing that's ever happened to her.*

Madge invited them out onto the terrace where she had coffee and bagels.

"You know, Madge," Suzy started, "It's perfectly normal to be nervous about getting married."

Madge stopped her short. "This isn't about getting married. I've never been more sure of anything in my life than marrying Jason. Although a quiet little wedding would have sufficed, but Jason's handling all the details, and the family-and-friends-wedding-thing is important to him."

"Well, then what's got you in such a knot?" asked Trish.

"It's this Jack Feldy thing. Heather gave me a heads-up that she was suing Jack, and told me the entire disgusting story of what she went through. She also knew it would be just her word against the all-powerful Jack machine, and she asked me if he had ever done anything similar to me or anyone else at the network that I knew of. I told her I couldn't help her. And now I realize how wrong that is. I have to step forward."

"Step forward? You don't mean...on my God, Madge, did that pig harass you too?" asked an outraged Suzy.

Madge then told them the story. "When I first started at the network, Jack was the producer of the *Good Morning New York* show and I was just a news reader. And it started the same way it did with Heather. Grabbing my ass in the hall, and always standing a little too close when he talked to me. Then he'd ask me into his office to discuss my future at the network, and insist I close the door. It would start off innocently enough, but then the conversations would always end with some kind of proposition. Once he even threw a hotel room key at me and suggested I be there at noon for an afternoon delight."

"Oh, Madge. Why didn't you ever tell us this was going on?" said a shocked Suzy.

"I was too humiliated to discuss it with anyone. And I thought I had it in control, until one day he invited me to a 'meeting' in his new office. By now he was an executive VP at the network and had wrangled a big corner office. When his assistant called and said the meeting was at 8:00 p.m., a few bells and whistles went off, but then she said, 'Listen, on the QT, I think Jack is considering you for the anchor desk.'

"I arrived a little before eight. She said Jack was on the phone and she had to leave, but to just wait a few minutes and then knock on his door. He was expecting me.

"I knocked and Jack's booming voice said to come in and close the door. I walked in, but he wasn't there. Then he shouted out to open the door on the right and come into his conference room. I opened the door and was shocked that it was a bathroom and there was that bastard in the shower. He opened the door in all his glory and invited me to join him."

"What did you do?" asked a horrified Trish.

"I told him I'd be back in a second. I walked to his desk and grabbed a letter opener. And then I went back into the bathroom and told the bastard that if he ever bothered me again, I'd tell his wife after I cut his dick off with a letter opener. He laughed, and said his wife would never believe a little hussy like me. But then I reminded him that my mother and his wife had gone to grade school and high school together, and had been best friends up until the day my mother died. That was before Jack married her, so he never met my mother.

"'So you see,' I told Jack, 'if I tell your wife, she will definitely believe me and you will be dickless.' He never bothered me again. And I spent years trying to forget what he did ever happened."

Suzy and Trish both came over and embraced her. "I wish you had told us what you were going through," said Suzy. "So now what?"

"I'm going to head up to the farm this afternoon and tell Jason the whole story. And then I will call Heather and tell her my story and that I am willing to tell it to her lawyers and the world. And I'm sorry, Trish and Suzy. This will definitely cause a media storm for all of us. And the timing sucks with the wedding and the adoption too. I don't need to be the front page story right now."

"You have nothing to be sorry about, Madge Thompson. You need to stop this bastard from doing this ever again," said Trish.

"And you need to stay at the farm next week too," added Suzy. "It will be harder for the press to track you down there. And then you'll be in Africa, and hopefully by the time you return, there will be some new media scandal, and this will be yesterday's news."

***

Madge told Jason everything that night at the farm. She'd never seen Jason angry.

"I want to tear that bastard from limb to limb. Guys like him are slimy predators. We need to take him down. And how could you ever think I would think less of you? You were only in your twenties and this guy had all the power." He then took Madge in his arms and held her for a long, long time.

Madge was glad she had taken Suzy's advice to stay on the farm. By Monday afternoon the story broke that "Respected journalist Madge Thompson comes forward with her story of sexual harassment at the hands of Jack Feldy." Suzy called and told her reporters were camped outside the loft. She and Trish had been saying "no comment" to all.

By Wednesday, ten more women had come forward. By Friday, Jack Feldy had resigned and the lawyers were talking settlement numbers with the network. Karma, baby, Karma.

40

FROM THIS DAY FORWARD

It was a perfect fall day for a wedding. Jason and Madge were married under the gazebo in the flower garden that had been planted with mums in every color, daisies, and sunflowers, surrounded by family and their dearest friends.

Madge looked stunning. She wore an elegant strapless beige lace dress, with a full tea-length skirt. She was wearing a diamond heart pendant that opened with photos of Yonas and Jason inside, a wedding present from Jason. She carried a small bouquet of white hydrangeas.

Trish had shopped her closet, which she now enjoyed doing, and wore an emerald green satin empire dress that was perfect with her beautiful red hair. Suzy was in a burnt orange short crepe sheath that showed off her long legs.

Chrissy was the third bridesmaid, and wore a teal blue silk dress, with a wide skirt and a big belt that showcased her tiny waist and beautiful blue eyes.

A harpist played "If Ever I Would Leave You," as Madge walked down the aisle to a beaming Jason.

Celeste turned to the other Ripe Tomatoes at the end of the ceremony and said, "This was more romantic than any one of my best-selling romance novels."

Hope chimed in with, "Now wipe those tears, Tomatoes, we don't want mascara running down our cosmetically plumped-up cheeks."

The reception and dinner were set up buffet style, which allowed everyone to mingle and walk around. Jason had hired the jazz band that was playing at the restaurant the night he ran into Madge and the other two spa runaways. When the band started playing "Unforgettable", he grabbed Madge and they whirled around the patio together.

Jason's mom and dad both made eloquent toasts and welcomed Madge into their family. "And we can't begin to tell you how excited we will be to meet our grandson shortly too." That brought tears to everyone's eyes.

As the evening was ending, Chrissy reminded Madge that she had to throw the bouquet. All the single Ripe Tomatoes got in the center, with Hope laughing, "God help the next guy who marries one of us," and winked at Marvin. They all cheered when Celeste caught the bouquet.

***

Suzy came downstairs the next morning to find John in the kitchen preparing breakfast. "I figured I'd give Jason a break this morning," he said as he winked.

He is one sexy man, Suzy thought to herself. "So, John, are you ready to be famous again? The Arpello campaign launches just before Thanksgiving."

"And we have high hopes that you'll sell millions of bottles of perfume for us again," said Margot as she entered the kitchen too.

"I don't know how I let you ladies talk me into this. But I have to say, it's kind of fun."

Eventually, everyone straggled down to the kitchen for coffee and omelets, with Madge and Jason making their entrance last.

They were both dressed and ready to head to the airport. "We can't thank you enough for being here with us this weekend," Madge said, "and forgive us for leaving so soon today, but we're off to see our son."

Suzy and Trish looked at each other and smiled. They had never seen Madge so happy.

41

PAYING RESPECTS

It was Tuesday morning after the long weekend, and Trish and Suzy were having trouble getting back into work mode. They had spent the better part of the morning reliving the highlights of Madge and Jason's wedding.

"Well, I better work on getting those workshop schedules posted," said Trish. As she was heading down the spiral staircase to talk to their webmaster, her cell rang. Five minutes later she was back in the conference room in tears.

"Trish, what on earth..."

"It's Tania. She died in her sleep last night."

"Oh no," said Suzy, and she started crying too.

By the end of the day, Trish had found out that Tania's family was flying her body to Jamaica where she would be buried with her family and ancestors later that week.

"Suzy, I'd really like to go to the funeral. It will only be a couple of days. Do you think you can handle things here without me?"

"Of course. Yes, you must go. And we'll check in and make sure Michael's okay too."

***

It had been a beautiful and moving service. As the plane took off from Montego Bay heading back to New York, Trish said a silent farewell to her friend. Tania's family had graciously welcomed her into their family and thanked her over and over for giving Tania's art the showcase it needed.

The day after the funeral, Tania's three sisters invited her to their family home for dinner. It was then that they told her about the letter with Tania's last requests, one of which involved Trish.

"She wanted you to have her last collection of paintings, which she calls *Happiness*," said her sister Rosie. "They are in her apartment. Here is the key. We hope they will find a home in your gallery."

Trish was overwhelmed. "But those should be yours," she insisted.

"No, no. They belong to you now. That is what Tania wanted. And she is always here with us," said Rosie as she spread her hands around the room whose walls were adorned with Tania's art.

Trish was now thinking about the gallery. Yes, they should be there, but how could she ever go back there? She was glad to be heading home to Michael and glad it was a weekend too.

***

"It seems so strange not be greeted by Tania," Trish said to Michael. Shortly after they finished breakfast Sunday morning, they had called an Uber and were now inside Tania's apartment. "Tania converted the end bedroom to a studio because it has great light," she said as they walked down the hallway.

On the floor, lining the walls, were canvases in a variety of sizes. As Trish started to go through them, her excitement was palpable. "Michael, this is the best work she has ever done. And *Happiness* is the perfect name." There were seascapes, and landscapes, and flowers and birds in swirls of glorious color. You couldn't help but smile, just looking at them.

Trish sat on the floor in the middle of the room, looking from one canvas to the next.

Michael sat down next to her. "These are exquisite, Trish. But what are you going to do with them?"

After a long pause, Trish replied, "There's only one thing I can do."

***

It was a perfect late October evening. There was a little nip in the air and the sunset turned the sky into beautiful hues of pinks and blues and oranges. "It looks like one of Tania's canvases," Suzy said to Ken as they walked into the gallery.

Madge and Jason were there already, and Trish rushed over to greet Suzy and Ken.

"What do you think?" asked Trish.

Suzy and Ken looked around the room at the dazzling display of Tania's last paintings. "It's breathtaking," said Suzy. "What a wonderful tribute to Tania."

Within the next hour, the gallery was standing room only as Tania's family and many friends poured into the gallery to memorialize her, along with some of New York's elite art collectors.

With the room full and a line outside, a screen lowered from one of the walls and a moment later there was Tania, filling the screen. It was a clip from the interview Madge had done with Tania in January.

"Honey, we're all remarkable. All you have to do is keep living, keep breathing, and keep looking inside you for what makes you happy and then do it. Happiness isn't something other people

bestow on you. If you're waiting for that, you'll be dead and gone. Everything you need to make you happy is right in here," said Tania as she pointed to her heart.

There was thunderous applause and a lot of people who knew Tania were dabbing at their eyes.

At the end of the evening, Trish took the microphone. "I want to thank you all for being here tonight and celebrating the life of the remarkable Tania — and yes, she was remarkable — and her glorious art. Tania would have been overwhelmed to know that her paintings tonight have sold for over one million dollars that will be donated to start an art and music program in the small parish school that Tania attended as a child, to encourage young girls to dream big, and find their happiness."

After everyone had left the gallery, Suzy, Ken, Madge, and Jason raised glasses to toast Trish and Michael. "Well-done," said Ken.

"Thank you," said Trish. "And here's to exorcising the evil that was in this gallery that is now filled with light, love, and happiness."

42

GRATEFUL

It was the start of Thanksgiving week and Suzy, Madge, and Trish were on pins and needles. The Arpello campaign was previewing at The Three Tomatoes for a three-day exclusive before it went nationwide with a broadcast campaign that was launching Thanksgiving Day, just in time for Black Friday.

They had sent out a series of teaser ads in their daily newsletters (and to the media). The eblast would drop at noon with the subject line Remember Your First Time?. The body of the email was the black-and-white print ad featuring John, the Arpello man, wearing his famous white shirt with a few unbuttoned buttons.

He looked as sexy as he did thirty years ago. The tagline said Aprello, You Never Forget Your First. It linked to the beautiful video spot that opened with an image of a young John and a young woman and then morphed into today's John walking along the beach, hand in hand with a beautiful woman with long silver hair. There was an exclusive offer to buy Arpello at The Three Tomatoes.

"I'm sorry we'll miss the Thanksgiving excitement at your house, Suzy, when the first ad comes on the air," said Madge, "but we haven't seen Yonas in over a month. I don't know when I'll be able to get cell service but keep sending me emails and texts with the campaign updates. We leave tonight, but we'll be back early next week." And then sighing, "Another trip when we'll be returning without him."

It had been an agonizing time for Madge and Jason. Even with their friends in high places, cutting through the red tape of adoption was not an easy process.

"Oh, sweetie," said Suzy putting her arms around Madge. "Hopefully it won't be long now."

Before Madge and Jason even left for the airport, social media was lighting up with #RememberYourFirstTime with links to the video. "Well looks like Dad's a heartthrob again," laughed Jason as they headed to the airport.

Trish and Michael arrived at Suzy and Ken's earlier than usual on Thanksgiving Day. The first Arpello spot was scheduled to run just before Santa would arrive at Macy's Thanksgiving Day Parade.

Trish and Suzy were still ecstatic about the sales of Arpello during the exclusive three-day offer at The Three Tomatoes. The traffic surge had actually crashed the website the first day. Their web team had stayed up half the night getting everything back up and running.

Keri was home from school and joined them all in the den. Ian, Emily, and baby Elsa were joining them for dessert. Suzy realized she'd have to get used to sharing Ian on holidays.

They all settled in to watch the big screen TV, and shortly before noon, with Joe Cocker's distinctive voice singing, "You are so beautiful," John Madison's handsome face appeared on screen.

"Wow," said Keri. "For an old dude, he's really hot. Mom, let me try that perfume."

Keri went upstairs to Suzy's dresser to spritz herself, and Michael joined Ken in the kitchen.

Suzy poured a glass of wine for Trish and herself. "I think we did it."

Later that afternoon, as Ian and Emily joined them for dessert, while the baby slept peacefully in her car seat, Suzy looked around the table and realized how much she had to be grateful for. *What a difference a year makes,* she thought.

On Saturday morning Suzy's cell rang and Margot's number popped up. She took a deep breath before answering. She was nervous, because she knew there were a lot of great ad campaigns that never sold products. "Margot, Happy Thanksgiving."

"Well," replied Margot, "you have certainly made mine a happy one. I just got the Arpello sales report and while it's still early, this is the most successful first day launch sales we have ever had."

***

Madge was grateful too this Thanksgiving Day. Yonas had flown into her arms the second he saw her, and said, "Mommy, I love you" in English. She and Jason had hired a teacher for the orphanage to teach Yonas and the other children English, and Yonas was making amazing progress. They were also excited that the new wing they were financing was almost completed. And they had equipped the courtyard with a swing set and bought more sports equipment. While they couldn't adopt all the children, they could make life at the orphanage a little better for them.

The most difficult part, as always, was leaving Yonas. He clung to her and the director had to literally pry him off. "I don't know how much more of this I can take," Madge said through her tears to Jason.

"I know, sweetheart. I know."

43

HOLIDAY SURPRISES

"Well, here's to us," said Trish as the trio clinked their martini glasses.

"And here's to feeling on top of the world," added Suzy. They had decided to treat themselves to martinis at Bar SixtyFive, the cocktail lounge on the sixty-fifth floor of 30 Rockefeller Center, before their Ripe Tomatoes holiday dinner. "And I hope we're expensing these drinks because we could each own a pair of Manolo Blahniks at these prices."

"Well, we deserve it," said Madge. "This last year's been a hellava ride."

"Any updates on Yonas?" asked Trish.

"I think we're getting closer, but it looks like we won't get him here until sometime in January now. So, we'll be heading to

Ethiopia a few days before Christmas. I really wanted Yonas to spend his first Christmas with us here this year," Madge said wistfully.

"But what a difference a year makes," said Suzy. "Last Christmas you were heading to Aspen."

"And Michael and I were separated," said Trish.

"And you got canned just before Christmas," said Madge to Suzy.

They started laughing. "Yep, we do deserve to be on top of the world."

***

The Gramercy Tavern was the venue for this year's Ripe Tomatoes holiday dinner, and Hope had made sure to get them a table that strategically placed them in a "let's be seen" spot. As the producer of one of Broadway's top hits of the season, Hope was enjoying every second of much deserved adulation. And even the tourists who had no idea who any of them were couldn't help but notice this attractive, vibrant, elegantly dressed group of women.

Hope, as usual, had some delectable gossip to share. "Ellen Martin's husband has left her for a sweet young thing."

"Really, and who is she?" asked Mimi.

"Well, that's the juicy part. It's not a she...it's a he." Hope always knew how to deliver a great bombshell. Then she filled them in on the who and where. The who was a much younger actor/dancer who had a lead role in Ellen's last show. The where is Ellen arriving home early from a West Coast trip to find them in her bed in the heat of passion. "If she wasn't the ultimate bitch, I'd almost feel sorry for her."

Celeste regaled them with her latest dating adventures. "Well, I figured since I caught Madge's bouquet, I better get back out there."

And they all oohed and ahhed over Marilyn's engagement ring — it was the biggest diamond any of them had ever seen. Marilyn was a little vague about what he did for a living, and Suzy just hoped he wasn't another gold digger, like hubby number one.

They discussed their holiday plans. Arlene had decided to take a cruise by herself, just for a little respite. It was too sad to visit her husband who didn't know who she was anymore.

And of course, the entire group wanted to see the latest photos of Yonas.

As Suzy headed home that night, she realized how much she loved this group of women. She was looking forward to Christmas and the new year. She was only slightly concerned with the message she received just before they headed out for drinks from her gynecologist's office to please call in the morning.

***

Suzy was putting the finishing touches on the buffet table. It was Christmas Eve. Her kids were home, and Trish and Michael were joining them for dinner. A couple of days before, she called to invite Margot Tuttinger.

"I'm sure she'll have plans," she had said to Trish earlier that week, "but I thought it would be lovely to have her join us and also celebrate the success of Arpello."

To her surprise, not only did Margot say yes, but she asked if Jason's parents could come along as well, since they were her guests in the city this year. They had hopes that Jason and Madge would have Yonas home to spend his first Christmas in New York. When they learned that wasn't happening, they decided to stay in the city anyway. Suzy was delighted. And the more people she had around her, the better. It might take her mind off the news she was going to have to tell Ken right after Christmas.

Margot arrived with a huge basket of every beauty product her company made. John brought two bottles of Veuve Clicquot, and Elizabeth had a box of Christmas cookies she had baked herself.

Ken poured champagne for all of them and toasts were made around the room.

"And I want to thank Suzy, Trish, Madge, and John for bringing back Arpello, and proving that women over forty still matter to the beauty industry," added Margot.

Suzy thanked them all for joining them for Christmas Eve. "You have no idea how special it is to have you all here tonight. The only thing that could make tonight more perfect would be to have Jason, Madge, and Yonas here too."

They all toasted to that and Suzy invited them to the buffet table. They were just about to start on desserts when they heard the front door open, and "Ho, Ho, Ho", as Jason walked in the door. "Merry Christmas, everyone."

They were all stunned and delighted. "Where's Madge?" asked Suzy.

"Oh, she's bringing our Christmas present in."

And with that, Madge walked into the room, holding the hand of a little boy who was shyly trying to hide behind her.

"Meet Yonas."

The room erupted in happy pandemonium. Yonas was clinging to Madge, somewhat overwhelmed by his new extended family. They all finally settled down, and Madge and Jason told them how overjoyed they were when they got to the orphanage to the news that the adoption had been approved. "We signed a few papers, and left as soon as we could."

Yonas had been sitting on Madge's lap the entire time, and an hour later he was fast asleep. Jason gently carried him into the den and settled him on the couch, and Suzy, who had followed, put a blanket over him. She then leaned over and gave him a kiss on his forehead. "What a joy," she whispered.

When she and Jason returned to the living room, there were choruses of "He's beautiful. He's perfect. We're actually grandparents. We're aunts. We love him."

When Ken climbed into bed that night, he wrapped his arms around Suzy and said, "I think this is the most perfect Christmas ever." She was glad she had decided to wait until after Christmas to tell him her news. *At least he can have this perfect moment,* she thought.

44

BURY ME IN LOUBOUTINS

The day after Christmas, Suzy knew she couldn't put it off any longer. She had waited for Keri to leave the house to catch up with her friends, and walked into the den where Ken was reading the papers.

"Ken, I have something to tell you," she said as she moved the papers off the ottoman and sat next to him.

"Don't tell me you're leaving me," Ken said jokingly, and then realized by the look on Suzy's face that she had something serious to say. "Honey, what is it?"

"Well, you know I've had some heavy bleeding lately. I thought it was just menopause stuff, but I went to see my gynecologist, and she ran some tests." She paused, trying to compose herself. "Ken, I have uterine cancer."

Ken went pale. "Oh my God. When did you find this out?"

"A couple of days before Christmas."

"And you waited to tell me?" Ken said in shock.

"I didn't want to ruin Christmas."

He pulled her into his arms. "Tell me everything."

Suzy told him what she knew so far. "I have an appointment at 11:00 a.m. tomorrow with an oncologist at Memorial Sloan Kettering."

"I'm going with you."

***

They had been in the waiting room for an hour and a half and still had not been called in to see the doctor yet. Ken had gone to the desk every fifteen minutes to inquire. He came back to sit next to Suzy and took her hand. Their anxiety was already sky-high and the long wait was making it worse.

"Maybe we should be talking to a different doctor," Ken said.

"The wait is awful, but I think they're always dealing in crisis here, and my doctor was able to get me squeezed in to see Dr. Yoon," said Suzy. "And she's considered one of the top doctors in her field."

Finally, after a two-hour wait, they were escorted into Dr. Yoon's office.

"Listen, I know you're nervous, and *cancer* is a scary word. But we think yours is early stage, Suzy, and one with a good long-term outlook."

Relief flooded over Suzy and Ken. She then proceeded to tell them that the best option would be a full hysterectomy. And during the surgery, which they would do laparoscopically so she'd have a quick recovery, they would take several tissue samples and biopsy the lymph nodes. "Then we can determine where to go from there. We could get you scheduled this week, and you should be home for New Year's." Before they left the hospital, Suzy got all the necessary presurgery tests and was scheduled to return in three days for the hysterectomy.

Suzy and Ken talked it over that night, and decided they had to tell the kids. "But we'll just tell them it's a hysterectomy. We don't have to mention the *C* word yet. And I'll tell Trish," said Suzy, "but I don't want to tell Madge yet. She and Jason are in Vermont enjoying Yonas, and I don't want to distract from their joy."

After Suzy told Trish she was really glad she did. Ken was a wreck and she couldn't really express her fears to him. But Trish was calm, listened to Suzy's fears, and then, based on all the research she had quickly done, helped to soothe her.

Trish was there with Ken the day of the surgery, to help keep him calm. "Suzy's my life, and I can't imagine a day without her," he said as Trish put a reassuring arm around his shoulders.

The surgery went fine, and Dr. Yoon gave Ken and Trish a thorough post-op report. "So far everything looks good, and the lymph nodes look clean, but of course we have to wait for the full pathology to come back, and with the holidays that will take a few days. I'll look in on her tomorrow morning, and if all looks good we'll send her home."

Trish arrived at Suzy's home at noon on New Year's Eve, laden with food from her favorite organic grocer. She had bone broth, a broccoli and cauliflower casserole, and fresh blueberries for dessert. "They're all good cancer-fighting foods," Trish said to Suzy, and they sat down to eat in the kitchen nook.

"I really think you should tell Madge," Trish said.

"I know. I will, but let's wait until I get all the results back next week. There's no reason to bother her now. And, Trish, thanks for being here. I'm glad you're going with us when the test results come in. I know I can count on you to ask all the right questions."

***

The next few days were agony, and it was almost a full week before they heard from Dr. Yoon's office that the pathology was back.

"Sarcoma." That was the dreaded word Dr. Yoon delivered. She explained that they are two types of uterine cancers. Adenocarcinoma develops from the cells in the endometrium, and usually accounts for 80 percent of uterine cancers. But sarcoma, which develops in the uterine muscle is rarer, and potentially more serious.

"What's the next step, and do I need further treatment?" Suzy managed to ask.

"The good news is that with the hysterectomy, the tumor is gone. And there are no signs of cancer in any of the lymph nodes or the tissue samples we took. If we were dealing with adenocarcinoma, I wouldn't recommend any further treatments, just close monitoring. But sarcoma can be a potentially deadly cancer. And while we could do monitoring, it's my recommendation that you do six weeks of radiation and chemotherapy. But at this point, the decision is yours."

Trish piped in, "Well, what about the side effects and long-term risks associated with radiation and chemotherapy? Wouldn't monitoring be a better option?"

"You raise a very good point. There's a trade-off, and this is not a black or white scenario. Please give this serious consideration, Suzy. You might also want a second opinion, and I am here to answer your questions, anytime."

Back at the house, Suzy looked at Trish and Ken. "How the hell am I supposed to make this kind of decision?"

"Well, I think a second opinion is definitely a good next step," said Ken.

And thanks to all of Trish's connections, by the end of the day Suzy had an appointment for the next morning with another highly regarded gyno oncologist.

After reviewing all the files and reports, his recommendation was that he didn't think radiation and chemo were warranted, and they should just do close monitoring.

It was another sleepless night for Suzy and Ken. "Ken," Suzy pleaded, "please tell me what you think I should do?"

"Oh, sweetheart," he said and took her in his arms. "We've talked to two highly regarded doctors with differing opinions. And there's a case to be made either way. All I know is that I want to grow very old with you, but only you can make this decision."

The next morning Suzy called Dr. Yoon and asked if she could see her. "Yes, come at the end of the day, and that way I'll have more time for you."

This time Suzy opted to go alone, and at 6:00 p.m. the next day, she was seated across from Dr. Yoon. She told her about the second opinion. Dr. Yoon agreed that was definitely a less aggressive option, and one she would support if that was Suzy's decision.

"But please, Dr. Yoon, I really need you to answer this question. If this were you, what would you do?"

Dr. Yoon waited, and after what seemed like an eternity, said, "Suzy, I would go for the radiation and chemotherapy. While all the reports look good, all it takes is one rogue cancer cell, and you could be looking at a second, potentially killer, cancer. I wouldn't want to take my chances and be scared every time I had to come in for a cancer screening."

By the next morning, Suzy had made up her mind. She told Ken over breakfast. "I'm going with the radiation and chemo." And then she cried.

They told the kids that night. Suzy and Ken assured them both that she was going to be fine, and this was purely precautionary. "Will you lose your hair, Mom?" Keri asked.

"Probably, but it will grow back. And that's what wigs are for."

Keri and Ian hugged her, and she knew they were holding back tears. She was glad they were heading back to school in a couple of days.

***

It was the second week of the new year. Madge, Jason, and Yonas had returned to New York and were staying in Madge's apartment.

"We realized the loft penthouse isn't very kid friendly and there's only one bedroom. Although right now, Yonas has spent every night curled up between Jason and me. I'm sure he'll get more secure with time," Madge was explaining to Trish and Suzy before their status meeting. "And how were your New Year's celebrations?"

"Madge," began Suzy, "I have something to tell you." It was almost as difficult telling Madge as it was telling her children.

"You should have told me, Suzy. You know I would have been here with you, in a nanosecond."

"And that's exactly why I didn't tell you," said Suzy. "You needed time to bond with Yonas."

Suzy was scheduled for her first radiation treatment that week and her first chemo treatment the following week.

"Listen, Trish has introduced me to her friends at the integrated health center and they've been wonderful. I have a nutritionist who specializes in cancer-fighting foods and nutrition during chemo, plus an acupuncturist, a meditation specialist, and I have a prescription for marijuana — whoo hoo! So, I fully plan to work through this two months of hell. So, let's get on with the status report."

A few days after her second chemo treatment, she and Trish and Madge went upstairs to the loft's apartment, and they shaved her head. They all cried, and then Madge pulled out a beautiful long blond wig, handmade of human hair, and Suzy looked like Suzy again.

"Listen, I have one more request," Suzy said to her two best friends.

"Anything!"

"Bury me in my Louboutins." They all hugged and laughed.

When she walked in the door that night, Ken hugged her and didn't even realize it was a wig. It wasn't until he walked into the bedroom later that night and Suzy was sitting in bed with her bald head on display, that he realized what had happened.

She had tears streaming down her face, but managed to say through her tears, "Well, I guess you never thought you'd be sleeping with a bald lady."

Ken rushed to embrace her. "Suzy, you are beautiful with and without hair. The most important thing is for you to be healthy. I love you more than words can say. And you're the one who said it's only hair. It will grow back."

Suzy hugged him back. "Whatever would I do without you?"

45

THE LOST GENERATION

It had been only two months since Yonas's arrival and he was doing remarkably well. With the help of tutors, and a five-year-old's ability to soak up knowledge like a sponge, his English was almost on par with that of his peers. They enrolled him at the United Nations International School because it was known for its quality international education, and most important, it had a student body with diverse cultural heritages. He had classmates from all over the world, including Ethiopia.

Jason loved taking him to school every morning and picking him up each day. And Madge loved nothing better than coming home at the end of the day to her two guys. And although her "bachelorette pad" was a little better than Jason's one-bedroom loft, they had agreed to start looking for something a bit more suitable for a kid, toys, a kitchen you could actually cook and eat in, and some outdoor space. And if Jason and Yonas had their way, a dog too.

"Call Angela," Trish said to Madge. "She was great finding us our Harlem home."

Suzy laughed. "I never thought I'd see the day when you'd be looking for a place with a real kitchen. I remember when you use to use your oven to store your designer handbags."

They were in the loft conference room for their weekly status meeting. Remarkably, over the course of the past two months of treatments, Suzy had never missed one. And today they were celebrating her last chemo treatment with cappuccinos and deliciously sinful Magnolia Bakery cupcakes.

"So how does it feel?" Madge asked Suzy.

"It's the most glorious sense of freedom to be rid of noxious sessions of poisons coursing through my body. And I don't know how I can ever thank the two of you for all your support these past two months."

Madge and Trish had alternated being with Suzy for every one of her chemo sessions.

"Now I just hope my hair starts growing back along with my taste for wine and martinis," Suzy quipped. "Let's get down to business."

They had hired two ad salespeople, and with the success of the Arpello campaign launch at The Three Tomatoes, they were getting traction with other advertisers. And their monthly events were getting sponsors too.

"So, I really think we can pull off an all-day conference now with sponsors," said Suzy. "We can build content under the umbrella of 'That's *Not* All, Folks.' Our monthly event attendance keeps growing, and while we may not bring in five hundred people like Ginny Dalton's bullshit summit we went to a couple of years ago, I think we can get two hundred to three hundred people who want to be inspired about growing older and want credible information on health and wellness too."

Trish and Madge agreed.

"Great," said Suzy, "I think we should start planning this for the fall, which will give us time to find advertisers and sponsors, and a good lead time to promote it."

"Now, is everything set for the private screening next week?" Trish asked.

They were all excited. Madge had finished the documentary, their first Three Tomatoes film production.

After going through the nearly two hundred hours of footage they'd shot on their trips through Africa and other parts of the world, Madge had decided to focus on the real victims of war, poverty, and famine — the children. It was called *The Lost Generation.*

"I think so. We've got the screening room at the Greenwich Hotel, which holds one hundred. And I have confirmation from some of the top execs from cable and the streaming networks. Jason's parents are coming and so is Margot. And all the Ripe Tomatoes will be there too," said Madge. "Fingers crossed we get distribution."

"I don't know how any TV or film exec can watch it and not want to get it out there," said Trish. "It's documentary storytelling at its best."

"And you're not biased at all," laughed Madge.

"Speaking of the Ripe Tomatoes, Hope really wants us all at next month's dinner," said Suzy. "I told her I think I may be up to it by then."

"And as much as I love coming home to Jason and Yonas, they'll probably love a guy's night," added Madge. "I'm in."

"Me too," said Trish. "So, Suzy, that gives you a month to get your martini taste buds back."

***

Suzy and Trish had seen many cuts of the film along the way, mostly on their computers, but watching the final version of *The Lost Generation* on a big screen with an audience, and then seeing the credits roll up with "A Three Tomatoes Production," was a thrill. They were so enthralled watching the credits they didn't realize that everyone in the theater was on their feet applauding.

As soon as the credits ended Madge came out on the stage. "I want to thank you all for being here tonight. So many people were involved in the making of this film, our intrepid film crew, my Three Tomatoes partners and best friends, Trish Hogan and Suzy Hamilton, and the support of many organizations who talked to us and allowed us into places where many have not been before.

"But there are two people I want to thank who without their love, support, and inspiration, this film would not have happened. Let me introduce my amazing husband, Jason, and the little boy who stole our hearts, our son, Yonas." And with that, Jason and Yonas walked onto the stage hand in hand.

"Oh my gosh," whispered Celeste to Hope as they headed into the room next door for a reception, "that is the most precious child."

"I agree," said Hope, "and I don't even like kids."

Madge and Jason watched as everyone headed to the next room. "This was the perfect place to screen the film," Madge said to Jason. "It was your little surprise screening of *Ghostbusters* right here that enabled us to move forward. And look where that has led us." And she lifted Yonas in her arms for a huge hug.

Before the week was over, there was a bidding war to see who would get the rights to air *The Lost Generation*.

46

MORE WEDDING BELLS

"Well, here's to Brooklyn," said Suzy as she and Madge and Trish clinked martini glasses.

"I know," laughed Madge. "Whoever would have thought I'd be crossing the Brooklyn Bridge every day? But Cobble Hill is perfect. We're in a family neighborhood with parks and tons of kids. And Yonas will love the backyard and sidewalks to learn how to ride a bike too. And the brownstone has been fully renovated, although Jason already has some tweaking plans. With luck, we'll be in by the end of April."

"And I'm really looking forward to our Ripe Tomatoes dinner tonight," said Trish. "We haven't been to a dinner with them since December."

"Yes, we need to get caught up on all the news and gossip."

Dinner did not disappoint.

"Oh, we are so happy to have our Three Tomatoes back in the fold," said Hope. "Here's to love, happiness, and most important, health," she said as they all raised their glasses.

"And we were all profoundly moved by your brilliant film, Madge. Any updates?" asked Celeste.

"Well, fingers crossed," said Madge, "it looks like we have a deal with one of the big cable networks and the film could be on the air by June."

"Well, even more things to celebrate," said Hope.

They were soon busy catching up. Madge told them that thanks to Angela's real estate brilliance, they had found a perfect home in Brooklyn.

"And where is Marilyn tonight?" asked Trish. "She's the only Tomato missing."

Hope sighed. "Well, Marilyn isn't having very good luck in the man department. Turns out the 'man of her dreams' is an international scam artist who has conned dozens of wealthy women on every continent. Thank goodness Marilyn's brother got suspicious and hired a private detective to look at this guy's background before Marilyn walked down the aisle with him. Turns out the guy has two other wives on two different continents, and that big engagement rock was a very good zirconia."

"Oh, how awful for Marilyn," said Mimi. "How did she take the news?"

"At first she didn't want to believe it and was furious with her brother. But when she saw the evidence in black-and-white, she kicked the gigolo to the curb, packed a bag, and is recovering at a very exclusive spa in the South of France."

They talked for a few minutes about how bad they felt for Marilyn, who was kind and generous, but a bit too naive.

"But then there's our dear Celeste," said Hope, "who never has a problem in the man department."

They all looked toward Celeste who was smiling in silence.

"Just tell them," urged Hope.

"Well, Madge, turns out there is magic in catching the bridal bouquet. I hope you all like June weddings in London."

There were cries around the table for details, details, details, and most important who was the lucky groom.

"I'm sure some of you may know the name Sir Oliver Spence," said Celeste. That of course was an understatement, since Oliver Spence was one of the all-time top mystery writers in the world, who had a number one best seller every year for the past thirty-five years.

"We've known each other casually for years, of course. But this past fall we were both speakers at a writers' conference in London, and he invited me to dinner. His wife passed away a couple of years ago and he told me how lonely he had been and how nice it was to be in the company of a lovely woman. Well, one dinner led to three dinners in London, and then he invited me to his home about an hour outside of London. Well, *home* isn't quite the right word — it's actually a beautiful English country estate, with the most exquisite rose gardens. And ever since that weekend, he comes here for a week each month, or I go there."

"And then last month when I was visiting him he asked me to marry him."

"This sounds like one of your romance novels," said Arlene. "I'm so happy for you."

"Yes, I couldn't have written it better myself. And I want you all there."

With that, they ordered a bottle of champagne and they all pledged they wouldn't miss Celeste's wedding for anything.

47

WE'RE GOING TO BE FAMOUS

It had been an exciting spring for The Three Tomatoes.

Madge, Jason, and Yonas moved to Brooklyn and were loving it.

Suzy was getting stronger every day and was trying to live her life without waiting for the other shoe to drop.

It was early May and she and Trish were excited to be meeting with Jason at the small integrated health center that had been founded by Trish's friends. Today he was finalizing his plans to invest in them and expand their facility to a state-of-the art Integrated Women's Health Care Center that they hoped could become a replicable model.

"You know, Jason," Suzy said as they sat in the center's small conference room. "Now that I've personally experienced a serious illness, I understand how difficult it is to navigate the health care system. If it hadn't been for Trish and the resources you found for me here at the Center, I would have had a much more difficult time."

Jason nodded his head. "I know. I learned a lot about the obstacles with Abigail. The anxiety of the long waits in the waiting rooms. The interminable wait to get test results back. And the reluctance of traditional health care systems to incorporate alternative treatments as well. And it shouldn't only be the wealthy who can access leading edge and experimental treatments."

"Jason Madison, you are about to improve the lives of many, many women in New York City," said Taylor Cramer, the founder of the Center, as she signed their agreement.

Trish felt like she was walking on air as they left the Center. "You know Taylor is right, Jason. You're creating the future of what good health care should look like."

"Trish, I couldn't have done this without you and your impressive knowledge of the issues. And Suzy's experience mirrored Abigail's in many ways. Hopefully we're on the right path here. Well, it's almost time for me to pick up Yonas at school," he hugged them both, and off he went.

Trish and Suzy grabbed a cab to head back to the office. Just as they reached the loft and were getting out of the cab, Suzy's cell phone rang.

"Hey, Margot, great to hear from you."

Trish held the loft door open for Suzy as she listened to Margot. "Oh my God," she shouted, "that is fabulous news. And yes, yes, of course I'll be there!!"

Suzy just stood there for a moment. "Well, speak up, girl," said Trish, "What was that all about?"

"The Arpello campaign has been nominated for the highest award in advertising by the Cannes Lions Festival, and Margot wants me to join her team for the awards ceremony in France next month."

"Oh my God, wait 'til we tell Madge," said Trish. They rushed up the stairs with the good news for Madge and the entire Three Tomatoes staff. You could hear the whoops and hollering on the street.

Suzy couldn't wait to get home to tell Ken.

"And, sweetheart, the timing is perfect. We'll go to Cannes first, and then head to London for Celeste's wedding."

"Oh, Suzy. I am so proud of you," said Ken. He pulled her into his arms, and gave her a passionate kiss. That night they made love for the first time since Suzy's illness.

Suzy looked into Ken's loving eyes after their tender lovemaking, and started singing, "You make me feel like a natural woman."

***

Two weeks later, Suzy, Ken, Trish, and Michael were all in Brooklyn sitting in Madge's and Jason's family room. Jason had made them a great dinner, and had just poured after-dinner drinks. Yonas was sitting on the floor with his new best friend, a very rambunctious golden retriever they had rescued from a puppy mill.

And they were all settled in to watch the first broadcast of *The Lost Generation* on one of the country's biggest cable networks.

Yonas got so excited when he saw his face on the big TV screen. "Mommy, Mommy, look. I'm going to be famous." They all laughed.

And as the credits rolled with "A Three Tomatoes Production", Trish and Suzy shouted out, "Mommy, Mommy, I think we're going to be famous too."

Over espressos and cappuccinos, they discussed their upcoming travel plans.

"Ken and I head to Cannes for the mid-June awards ceremony, and then we'll meet Trish and Michael for a few days of fun in London before Celeste's wedding," said Suzy.

"And we'll be arriving in London from Ethiopia just before the wedding," said Madge. She and Jason were returning to the orphanage for the first time with Yonas as soon as school ended next week. He missed some of his friends there, and they wanted to see the newest additions to the orphanage too.

"Here's to safe journeys, a London reunion, and a wedding to look forward to," said Michael.

48

ANOTHER BRIDE, ANOTHER JUNE

Suzy and Ken had spent a couple of very romantic days in Paris before heading to Cannes. They stayed at the Ritz, ate at some of their very favorite restaurants, and enjoyed jazz at some small bars off the tourist track. They slept late, ordered room service, and made a lot of love.

"I wish we were back in Paris," Suzy said as she was getting dressed for the awards ceremony. "I'm so nervous. And I hate that I still have to wear this damned wig. It's a constant reminder of illness. Can you zip me?"

Ken just stood there looking at her. "Suzy, you are perfection. I wish you could see you the way I see you," he said as he zipped up her gown.

And she was perfection. She was wearing a red satin gown with a slit up the side that showed flashes of her gorgeous legs and her

Louboutins. The gown had a high neckline and a cape. It was sexy and elegant.

"You'll be the belle of the ball," Ken said.

"Well, at least I have the most handsome man in Cannes to escort me there," Suzy said, admiring Ken who definitely rocked a tuxedo.

The cocktail reception was a collection of the biggest names in advertising and their clients, along with the biggest ass-kissers in the business too. Suzy spied her old boss Ryan out of the corner of her eye. He was making the rounds and seemed to be lobbying for the ass-kisser award.

The bells chimed, signaling the end of cocktails, and they slowly made their way to Margot's table. She looked stunning in an exquisite black vintage Schiaparelli gown.

"Suzy, I have a feeling this is our night."

The evening was long, the crowd was boisterous and drunk, and the excitement was building toward the announcement of the Titanium Lions, the most coveted of all the trophies. This was the category Arpello had been nominated for.

The CEO of the Cannes Lions finally came to the podium to present the final award. "The Titanium Lions celebrates game-changers. This year's winner has created provocative, boundary-busting, envy-inspiring work. We are pleased to present the

Titanium Lions to Arpello Perfume for the most successful brand relaunch in the history of the beauty industry, and the guts to market it, unapologetically, to women over forty."

The applause was deafening as Margot and her team, including Suzy, all went on the stage. Margot made a lovely and gracious speech acknowledging everyone, and especially Suzy and The Three Tomatoes, and ended it with, "This award is for every woman over the age of forty who has been made to feel marginalized and invisible by our industry, by simply being ignored. Let this be a rallying cry to other marketers out there, can you see us now?"

Suzy knew she would hold this glorious moment in her memory forever. They gathered back in the massive lobby for after-dinner drinks, and relished in the congratulations. And just as Suzy and Ken were getting ready to head back to their hotel, Ryan rushed over.

"Suzy, I've been trying to get to you all evening, but you've been surrounded by well-wishers. I just want to say 'well-done' and admit what a fucking asshole I was for not listening to you. And by the way, you look really hot too."

"Well, I'll be damned," said Suzy as she and Ken got into their limo. "Hope and Gab were both right. Success and clothes are the best revenge."

***

Jason thought it would be fun to hire a vintage Rolls-Royce to drive them all to Oliver Spence's country estate, and they would arrive in grand style.

"Now I know what 'to the manor born' means," said Trish as they pulled in front of the impressive entrance to the Spence estate.

They were quickly escorted by a waiting cortege of men in tails and white gloves through the mansion's very long center hallway, passing by a spectacular marble circular stairway, to a beautiful outdoor patio where a bar had been set up and a string quartet was playing. Within minutes they were surrounded by Hope, Arlene, Mimi, and Marilyn, exchanging hugs and air-kisses. "Don't mess with the face," Hope laughed. Marvin was by her side looking very debonair in his tux.

"Well, ladies," said Arlene, once they were all holding a glass of champagne, "we have a lot of celebrating to catch up on. First, to Suzy and The Three Tomatoes for your award at Cannes. I wish I could have been there to see that, Suzy. And then to her our dear Hope and Celeste for winning the Tony for best musical." They all clinked glasses.

"Oh, and look," said Hope. "There's Joni Evans and Collin McDougal. They each won a Tony too. They flew in just for the wedding, and head back to New York tomorrow."

They looked around at the rest of the gathering crowd, and kept whispering the names of the 'who's who' from the literary, entertainment worlds, and a few royals too.

"I need a master class in how to find a man from Celeste," said Marilyn laughingly.

They were soon requested to head to the ballroom for the wedding ceremony.

The quartet started to play Pachelbel's *Canon in D*, and Celeste appeared, a vision in pale blue chiffon, escorted down the aisle by her son to her very handsome silver-haired groom.

It was a short and beautiful ceremony. They had written their own vows (of course), and they promised that whatever time they had left on this planet would be devoted to loving and cherishing each other every day.

The seven-course dinner was set up in an elegant tent on the beautiful grounds of the estate. Suzy looked around at the impressive gathering and whispered to Ken, "If they could see us now."

Celeste and Oliver made the rounds to every table. They were a spectacular-looking bride and groom, and could leave a lot of twentysomethings in the dust with their class and charm. When Celeste got to their table, she said, "How can I ever thank my Ripe Tomatoes? You are the best friends anyone could ask for. And make sure all you single Tomatoes gather around in the center in a few minutes. I'll be throwing my bouquet."

"I'd love a little of your magic," said Marilyn.

As the cake was being served, the band leader invited all the single ladies to the dance floor. "The bride is about to throw her bouquet."

"Well, I guess we have to get out there," said Hope, grabbing Marilyn and Mimi too.

A bevy of young women were already there, and Hope stood a little outside the circle.

"Now on the count of one, two, three." Celeste threw her bouquet and straight in to the arms of Hope.

Hope returned to the table with her bounty, and looked at Marvin and said, "Well, maybe it's about time you made an honest woman of me."

***

All the way back to London they couldn't stop talking about the wedding and the manor home.

When they arrived back at the Dorchester, where they were all staying, Madge and Jason asked Suzy, Ken, Trish, and Michael if they'd join them for a nightcap at the bar.

They settled into a banquet and Madge said, "We have an announcement. We're parents again. Her name is Bitania. She's three years old and beautiful. And she's here with us now in the suite with Yonas and a nanny."

Suzy and Trish jumped up to hug Madge first, and then Jason, followed by Ken and Michael.

"Oh my God, how did this happen?" asked Suzy.

"Actually, we've been working on it for a while. Jason and I really wanted Yonas to have a sibling. And this time, because we had already adopted Yonas, it was much easier to adopt Bitania. Our family is complete."

"This is better news than winning the Cannes Lions," said Suzy.

49

THE BIRTHDAY BASH

The summer had been anything but quiet. Madge and Jason had been spending most of the time in Vermont with their new family.

Since the publicity from the Cannes award, Suzy had been fielding dozens of requests from marketers who wanted advice on marketing to women over forty.

And Trish was overseeing the expansion of the integrated health center.

At an early July meeting, they talked about the challenges of keeping up with the growing demands of The Three Tomatoes, and staying involved with the things each of them most loved about the business. They were definitely experiencing growing pains.

"I've been thinking it's time for a new structure," said Suzy. "What we need is a CEO who can manage the day-to-day, and we'll be the oversight board, in addition to managing the pieces of the business we love. For me, that's the working with marketers piece. For Madge, it's film and video. And for Trish, it's health and wellness."

"That's brilliant," said Madge.

"So, do we launch a search for a CEO?" asked Trish.

"Well, actually, I think we have our CEO right under our nose," said Suzy. "Amy Cole has been with us from the start. She designed our logo, our first website, and she's really grown into an excellent manager in the past two years overseeing our expanding staff. And she just turned forty last month, which officially makes her a Tomato," chuckled Suzy.

Madge and Trish immediately rallied to the idea. "Let's do it," said Madge.

By the end of the week, Amy Cole had officially been named CEO of The Three Tomatoes.

Early August rolled around, and it was time for Suzy's first follow-up scans since she had completed radiation and chemo treatments.

She put on a good front for Ken, but confided her fears in Trish. "What if it's come back?"

Trish assured her she'd get an all clear, and volunteered to go with her.

They were both sitting in Dr. Yoon's little office at the hospital. "Well, Suzy, good news. Everything looks great. There is no sign of cancer anywhere."

Suzy said a silent little prayer of thanks.

"We'll see you in six months, just as a precaution," said Dr. Yoon. "Now off, go live your life."

"Let's get a glass of wine," she said to Trish.

They found a quiet little bar.

"Here's to good health, my dear friend," Trish said to Suzy.

They sat quietly sipping their wines. "You know I've been thinking," said Suzy. "It's about time I finally celebrated my fiftieth birthday. Now that I'm almost fifty-two, and especially after Michael almost dying, and my cancer, I realize I need to be grateful that I get a chance to celebrate another birthday, and not hide from it."

"Oh, Suzy, I love that idea. Please, please let me plan the fiftieth bash I wanted to plan for you when you turned fifty the first time. I'll work with Ken on it."

***

And so it was that on a beautiful late August night, Suzy's two best friends and their husbands, the Ripe Tomatoes and their guys, Margot, Jason's parents, and the staff of The Three Tomatoes, along with Ken, Keri, Ian, and Emily boarded a yacht for a sunset cruise and dinner around Manhattan.

Suzy's hair had grown into a cute pixie, so she had ditched the wig. "You know, I kinda like it short," she said to Madge and Trish. "I might just keep it this way."

Suzy was wearing a beautiful white summer linen dress that looked great against her sprayed-on tan and showed off her fabulous legs. Madge had never looked more beautiful and vibrant since becoming a mother. She was wearing white skinny jeans, a red, white, and blue stripped boatneck T-shirt, and thong sandals. And Trish had bought the cutest spaghetti-strapped sundress, her first dress purchase in two years, and was wearing four-inch espadrilles. Her beautiful red hair was tied up in a ponytail.

They were standing on the deck watching the sun set over Manhattan, martinis in hand, when Ken strolled up to them and said, "Here's to the beautiful young girls I met thirty years ago, and to the beautiful smart, passionate women you are today. I'm one hell of a lucky guy to have the three of you in my life."

"Well-said," added Michael as he joined in a toast to them. "And I'm just jealous you've know them for thirty years," said Jason as they all raised their glasses.

50

THAT'S NOT ALL, FOLKS

Madge and Jason had returned to the city for the start of the school year.

Madge, Trish, and Suzy continued to meet for weekly status reports at the loft, but now Amy was part of it. The new structure seemed to be working out well.

Amy gave an update on their big conference for October, "That's *Not* All, Folks."

"We're over our goal for sponsorships, and ticket sales are going well. We know that most of the ticket sales will come in the last week, so with two hundred tickets already sold, we're projecting that we'll hit five hundred. And the good news is that the Hilton can accommodate at least another two hundred fifty people if we go over."

They were excited with this news. "And I'm really glad we decided to keep the tickets affordable, so that real women can attend," said Suzy.

"The conference lineup has really come together," Amy said. "We have an opening speaker who is starting a movement to eradicate ageism. She has one of the most watched TED talks, so she'll be terrific.

"We have sessions on looking your best at every age and we're going to do some on-site makeovers. We have sessions on feeling your best at every age with some leading experts in health and wellness, and then a great panel on finding your what's next. And there's my favorite panel of women over eighty who, like Tania, just say yes to life and are doing amazing things. And then at the very end, Heather Stone will moderate a panel featuring the three of you."

"What, no five-hundred-dollar jade eggs to energize your vagina, and no vaginal steaming experts?" laughed Madge.

Amy gave her a quizzical look.

"I guess you had to be there," said Madge.

"Well, October is a busy month," said Trish. "Jason will be unveiling the new Integrated Women's Health and Wellness Center in mid-October. I can't believe how quickly this all came together."

"Well, that was mostly your doing," said Madge.

"Yes, but without the huge donation from Jason's foundation, this would never be a reality."

"Well, as they say, 'it's five o'clock somewhere' and it's actually five o'clock here," said Madge. "This status meeting calls for champagne. Let's go up to the loft terrace. Come join us, Amy."

***

The official dedication of the new Integrated Women's Health and Wellness Center was tonight, but Trish had arranged for press tours of the new center that afternoon.

"We were able to take over this new ten-story building here in Midtown and customize it for our needs. You'll see as we tour each floor, this is a true one-stop, women's integrated health center. We even have our own labs and the latest in medical testing equipment. And we've streamlined the testing process, so that patients typically get results back in twenty-four to forty-eight hours, not days. And with the grants and research money that Jason Madison's foundation offers, we've assembled some of the country's best medical professionals in integrated medicine. We've created a first of its kind in the country, and no one will be turned away."

The press was duly impressed, and Trish had staff members on hand on each floor to answer questions.

The dedication and reception were scheduled for 6:00 p.m. Trish walked into the beautiful auditorium they had built, which was perfect for health and wellness seminars, with smaller rooms for workshops — a long way from the gallery days.

She did a quick soundcheck to make sure they were all set for tonight.

Michael arrived early to soothe her nerves, followed soon by Madge and Jason and then Suzy and Ken.

By 5:45 the two-hundred-fifty-person auditorium was jam-packed.

At 6:00 p.m. sharp, Trish walked onstage and introduced Taylor Cramer, the director and founder of the Center. Taylor talked about how their small Center had received this enormous opportunity to realize its full vision because of the efforts of Trish and Jason.

Trish then walked back onstage to introduce Jason Madison and Madge Thompson.

After Jason thanked Trish and Taylor for making this a reality, he said the Madison Thompson Foundation was privileged to dedicate the new wellness center.

With that, four men wheeled out something very large to the middle of the stage. It was covered.

He and Madge made their way to the center of the stage. Each took a side of the cover, and lifted it to unveil a beautiful large marble slab that would be placed at the entrance of the building. In beautiful bold bronze letters, it read, "The Abigail Gordon Women's Integrated Health and Wellness Center."

Trish, who had moved to the first row to sit next to Suzy, gasped. "I gather you didn't know about this?" Suzy whispered to her.

"I had no idea," said Trish.

Later during the reception, Trish and Suzy were finally able to get Jason and Madge alone for a minute. "Well, that was quite a surprise, and a beautiful tribute," said Trish to Jason.

"Actually, it was Madge's idea. And yes, it is a perfect tribute to a beautiful woman."

Jason walked away to chat with someone, and Suzy said, "You never cease to amaze me, Madge Thompson."

When Trish and Michael got home, Michael opened a bottle of wine and joined Trish outside in their little courtyard.

"I want to toast my beautiful and extraordinary wife. What you have created is a lasting legacy. I am so proud of you."

"And I am so proud of you, Dr. Hogan, Endowed Professor. And I love our home, and our new life together."

***

The "That's Not All, Folks" conference sold out two days before the conference date. Trish, Madge, and Suzy were behind the stage looking out at the seven hundred women in attendance.

"Holy shit," said Suzy. "Let's hope we don't disappoint them."

As the day progressed, it was going better than they could have imagined. Trish, Madge, and Suzy had taken turns as emcees and panel moderators. But now it was their turn to be interviewed, as the last panel of the day, in a session called, "Almost Everything You Wanted to Know About The Three Tomatoes."

The audience had just returned from a fifteen-minute break. An off-stage announcer asked them to return to their seats, and then announced, "Please welcome international journalist, Heather Stone."

The audience warmly applauded. Heather had received several network news offers after the sexual harassment case died down. But she didn't want to go back to being a news anchor. She had truly been moved by Madge's film reporting of the crisis in Africa, and decided she wanted to become a foreign correspondent and report from various corners of the world. Her underground coverage of ISIS had recently won her an Emmy.

Heather walked onto the stage. After a few remarks about how excellent the conference had been, she said, "It is now my pleasure to invite back onto the stage, The Three Tomatoes, Trish Hogan, Suzy Hamilton, and Madge Thompson."

The three walked out to rousing applause.

Heather started off the conversation. "I know you've all been best friends since your twenties, but you each went off in different directions, and had very successful careers in advertising, journalism, and art. And then you came together in your fifties and started this phenomenon called The Three Tomatoes with tens of thousands of loyal followers around the country. What's the secret to this success and how did it all start?"

"Like most great ideas, it started over martinis," said Suzy laughing. "Or I should say, trying to get the attention of a bartender, who was fawning over a couple of models, to actually order the martinis. That was the first time we realized we had become invisible. And then over the course of about three months, a series of life events happened that drew us together to start The Three Tomatoes."

Madge piped in and said, "I was feeling irrelevant and marginalized in a career that had been my life and identity for twenty-five years, and when the network wanted to, in effect, demote me and renew my contract for less money, I just quit."

"I found out my husband's firm was going under the day before he closed it, and we were practically bankrupted," said Trish. She paused and then added, "We separated, and during that time my husband was shot and almost killed by a crazy obsessed woman he had gotten involved with."

"And I looked around the conference room of the ad agency I was working for and realized I was the oldest one in the room, and no one gave a damn what I thought. I was aging out. And before I could quit, I got canned. So, you might say, it was the perfect storm."

"You could have just had a big pity party and sat around eating bonbons and drinking wine," continued Heather, "but you turned your experiences into something big."

"Actually, I had that little pity party you just described," said Madge. "But Suzy and Trish rescued me, and we realized it wasn't just us. Women all over the country who were past forty were experiencing the same things — they felt invisible, often marginalized because they were growing older, and many were just giving up on their dreams, feeling like, 'I guess that's all, folks.'"

"But we knew just by looking around at all the fabulous women we know, just like all of you here, that life can be wonderful and rewarding at every age, and every stage of our lives," said Trish. "In fact, it can actually be better."

"The problem is that we live in a society that worships youth, and makes women feel 'less than' as we age," said Suzy. "We're told that aging is something that is 'anti' and we have to fight it to stay youthful. That's fueled the growth of the trillion-dollar beauty and cosmetic surgery industry. We've bought into the myths of being too old to do that, or wear this, or act like that. Growing old has become something to fear, instead of celebrating."

"And that really pissed us off," said Madge. "But we were also fortunate because we had each other to cheer us on and a group of wonderful women we lovingly call 'The Ripe Tomatoes' who always say yes to life, and are living extraordinary lives."

"And that was the spirit we wanted The Three Tomatoes to have," said Trish. "We wanted to create a place where women can bolster each other, be informed about health and wellness, get expert advice on beauty and style, foster smart conversations about the myriad of topics we care about, dream big, and have fun too."

There was rousing applause as Trish finished that last statement.

"Well, I'd say you've succeeded at that, ladies," said Heather. "Any final remarks?"

"Don't ever let anyone count you out, or make you feel marginalized, or worse, invisible," said Suzy.

And as the audience was on their feet applauding, waiters were going down the aisles handing out glasses of champagne.

Heather raised her glass, and said, "Here's to The Three Tomatoes and to grownup women everywhere. Hello, world, can you see us now?"

EPILOGUE

"It's so fucking hot, my panties are melting," said Madge as she joined Trish and Suzy for martinis at Balthazar, the scene of the "becoming invisible" crime. They both laughed.

"Well, you know I had to say that, darlings, and I don't get to use that word very often these days with two young kids around," Madge laughed with them.

"We ordered your drink," Suzy said as the waiter placed one perfect martini in front of Madge. And then she lifted her glass and said, "Madge, congratulations on the Emmy nomination for *The Lost Generation*. We are so proud of you."

"That news was a great way to start off a hot July day in New York City. It made it worthwhile leaving Vermont. But I wouldn't have missed the chance to catch up with my two best friends, and with 'The Ripe Tomatoes' at dinner tonight."

"And there's more good news to toast," said Trish. "Suzy passed her latest cancer screening with flying colors."

"It's been a year and a half now," said Suzy, "but I still get that pit in my stomach each time. But the second I walk into the Abigail Gordon Women's Integrated Health and Wellness Center, I'm surrounded by such positive energy, the fears go away."

Trish caught them up on the latest developments at the Center. And they had all reviewed Amy's latest updates on The Three Tomatoes. "We definitely made the right decision promoting her to CEO," Suzy said.

Madge had them all laughing at the antics of her two children. "And what's so great is I never think about dieting anymore. Just chasing those two around keeps the weight off."

Before they could continue catching up on their lives, the young, good-looking bartender appeared with three more martinis, "These are on the house. You're The Three Tomatoes, aren't you?" he said. "I saw you interviewed on that morning show last month. You really rocked it."

He continued talking to them and didn't even notice the two beautiful models at the other end of the bar who were trying to get his attention.

ACKNOWLEDGEMENTS

This book was inspired by all the fabulous women I am so privileged to know who proudly call themselves Tomatoes. I thank my husband, Stu Benton, aka "Mr. Tomato," for his enduring love, supporting my every endeavor, and encouraging me to write a book. I am deeply indebted to Judy Katz for nudging me to tell The Three Tomatoes story and for providing her professional counsel throughout the process. I am so grateful to Beth Goehring for her expert advice and enthusiasm, and for coming up with the perfect title. Beth also led me to Anne-Marie Rutella who edited the book.

To the "original" three tomatoes, who in addition to me include Barbara Shimaitis, Debbie Yount, and our fourth tomato, Peggy Conlon, thanks for being my muses. And to my dear friend Sandra Russo with gratitude for her loyal support over the years and for being my booster club. I couldn't ask for better friends.

To my partners at The Three Tomatoes, my beautiful and smart daughter, Roni Jenkins, my "sister" and bright light, LA editor, Debbie Zipp, our vivacious and fun San Francisco editor, Kim Selby, the bigger than life, Randie Levine-Miller, who brings the music, and Carol Davis, who believed in us from the very beginning, and left us way too soon. Many thanks to Betty Rauch and Margie Altschuler, The Three Tomatoes Hot List partners.

ABOUT THE AUTHOR

Cheryl Benton, aka the "head tomato," is founder and publisher of The Three Tomatoes, a digital lifestyle media platform for "women who aren't kids." Having lived and worked for many years in New York City, the land of size zero twentysomethings, she was truly starting to feel like an invisible woman. She created The Three Tomatoes as the antidote for invisibility. She is chief cheerleader for smart, savvy women who want to live their lives fully at every age and every stage.

She spent her first career in the NYC advertising agency business as a top executive at some of the largest agencies in the world. She has served on the boards of several non-profits supporting women and girls

She is a graduate of Adelphi University and a recipient of the "Distinguished Alumni Award". She was also inducted into the Business Marketing Hall of Fame, and named a top CEO by SmartCEO magazine. A wife, mother, and grandmother (her favorite title), she resides in New York with her husband and two dogs. *Can You See Us Now*? is her first novel.

If you enjoyed this book, please take a few moments to write a review at Amazon.

Visit **www.thethreetomatoes.com**

Made in the USA
Columbia, SC
05 February 2018